The Haunted Tower of London

The Edmundson Family Adventures, Volume 5

Mick Jobe

Published by Mick Jobe, 2024.

This is a work of fiction. Similarities to real people, places, or events are entirely coincidental.

THE HAUNTED TOWER OF LONDON

First edition. November 14, 2024.

Copyright © 2024 Mick Jobe.

ISBN: 979-8230810926

Written by Mick Jobe.

The Haunted Tower of London
The teens investigate ghostly sightings tied to stolen crown jewels.

The Edmondson Family: A World of Adventure

The Edmondson siblings aren't your average teenagers. Raised in a family that values curiosity, courage, and teamwork, they've travelled the world with their archaeologist parents, picking up unique skills and a love for adventure along the way. Now, with their parents often immersed in research, the five siblings find themselves stepping into the spotlight, uncovering secrets, solving mysteries, and facing dangers that most people wouldn't dare dream of. Whether it's cracking ancient codes, exposing high-tech conspiracies, or navigating hidden cities, the Edmondsons prove that there's no challenge too big when you work together.

Meet the Edmondson Siblings:

Emma Edmondson (17 years old)

The eldest and the natural leader, Emma is intelligent, confident, and resourceful. Her sharp mind and strong sense of responsibility make her the team's planner and strategist. She has a talent for languages, which often comes in handy during their travels. Emma has a knack for staying calm under pressure and keeping the younger siblings focused when things get tough.

Leo Edmondson (15 years old)

Leo is the tech whiz and gadget genius of the family. With a love for computers, hacking, and building devices, he's the one who can unlock digital mysteries and outsmart high-tech security systems. He's also a bit of a prankster, keeping the group's spirits high with his humour, even in the face of danger.

Sophie Edmondson (14 years old)

The adventurous free spirit, Sophie is fearless and full of energy. She's an expert at climbing, sneaking, and navigating difficult terrain, making her the group's go-to for daring stunts and physical challenges. Sophie's impulsive nature sometimes gets her into trouble, but her bravery and quick thinking often save the day.

Max Edmondson (13 years old)

Max is the bookworm and history buff of the family. Obsessed with ancient cultures and mythology, he's a walking encyclopaedia who can connect the dots in any historical puzzle. Although shy and introverted, Max's vast knowledge often provides the key to solving mysteries. He's the heart of the team, reminding everyone of the importance of family and curiosity.

Ava Edmondson (12 years old)

The youngest, Ava is small but mighty, with a talent for observation and a photographic memory. She notices the tiniest details that everyone else misses, whether it's a subtle clue or a suspicious character. Her optimism and boundless enthusiasm keep the team motivated, and her artistic skills often help in unexpected ways, like sketching clues or deciphering ancient symbols.

Series Theme and Dynamics:

The Edmondsons are bound together by their love for adventure and their belief that every mystery has a solution if you're willing to work for it. With Emma's leadership, Leo's tech skills, Sophie's daring, Max's knowledge, and Ava's keen eyes, they form an unstoppable team. Along the way, they explore exotic locations, uncover hidden truths, and learn valuable lessons about courage, teamwork, and the power of family.

The Tower of London loomed ahead, a centuries-old fortress brimming with secrets and shadows. Its grey stone walls had seen kings crowned, queens executed, and treasures guarded through the ages. But as the Edmondson family approached its gates on a crisp autumn morning, they had no idea they were stepping into one of its most chilling mysteries yet.

For Emma, Leo, Sophie, Max, and Ava Edmondson, life was rarely ordinary. Raised by archaeologist parents who travelled the world uncovering history's secrets, the siblings had grown up learning to face danger, solve puzzles, and think on their feet. Each of them brought something unique to the table—Emma's leadership, Leo's tech skills, Sophie's daring, Max's deep knowledge, and Ava's sharp eye for detail. Together, they were an unstoppable team.

This time, though, they weren't on a daring expedition to uncover a lost city or crack an ancient code. This was supposed to be a simple family outing, a rare break from their usual whirlwind adventures. But as they crossed the Tower's threshold and heard whispers of ghostly sightings and missing Crown Jewels, the siblings realized that fate had other plans.

The stories spoke of a spectral figure haunting the Tower's shadowy corridors, of guards who swore they heard chilling whispers in the night, and of an ancient curse tied to the stolen jewels. What began as curiosity quickly turned into something much bigger—and far more dangerous.

Little did the Edmondsons know, this would be one of their most thrilling challenges yet. To uncover the truth, they'd have to rely on their wits, their courage, and above all, each other. Because at the Tower of London, secrets are never far from the surface—and some of them refuse to stay buried.

This is the story of a family of adventurers, a centuries-old mystery, and a haunting that would lead them into the very heart of history. Welcome to The Haunted Tower of London.

Chapter 1: Arrival at the Tower

The cobblestones underfoot seemed to hum with history as the Edmondson family approached the ancient gates of the Tower of London. The morning air was crisp, the faint tang of the River Thames lingering in the breeze. Against the backdrop of London's bustling streets, the Tower stood steadfast, a monument to centuries of intrigue, power, and mystery.

Emma Edmondson, the eldest of the five siblings, adjusted her scarf and glanced up at the looming stone walls. Despite the countless historical landmarks they had visited around the world, the Tower's aura of timelessness sent a shiver down her spine.

"It's so... old," Ava, the youngest, whispered, her wide brown eyes taking in the fortress.

"That's kind of the point," Max replied, not looking up from his well-worn guidebook. At thirteen, Max was the family historian, always armed with facts and trivia about their latest destination. "Did you know it was built by William the Conqueror in 1066? It's been a royal palace, a prison, and even a mint."

"Don't forget the place where they executed people," Sophie added with a grin, her fourteen-year-old thrill-seeker energy bubbling up. "I bet there are ghosts."

"You always think there are ghosts," Leo, fifteen, said, rolling his eyes. "It's probably just creaky floors and overactive imaginations."

"Or both," Emma said, nudging Leo. "Come on, let's not make a scene before we even get inside."

Their parents, Dr. Eleanor and Dr. James Edmondson, led the way through the main gates, pausing briefly to check in with a guide. Both archaeologists, their work often brought them to places like this, though usually without much time for sightseeing. This trip was an exception—a rare opportunity for the whole family to explore one of England's most iconic landmarks together.

"I want you kids to stay together," Dr. Eleanor said, her voice firm but warm. "Your dad and I have a meeting with the curator about the upcoming artifact exhibit. It shouldn't take long, but while we're working, you can enjoy the tour."

Dr. James smiled at his children. "Just don't wander too far. The Tower's big enough to get lost in, and I'd prefer not to spend the afternoon searching for you."

Emma nodded, instinctively stepping into her role as the leader of the group. "We'll stick together, promise."

The family passed through the gates, where a Yeoman Warder, clad in traditional uniform, greeted them with a booming voice.

"Welcome to the Tower of London! This fortress has stood for nearly a thousand years, guarding the secrets of kings, queens, and traitors alike!"

"Secrets, huh?" Sophie whispered to Leo. "Sounds promising."

As the guide continued, the siblings fanned out slightly, each taking in the sights in their own way. Max lingered by a plaque detailing the history of the White Tower, while Ava stopped to sketch a nearby raven, her small notebook already filling with quick pencil strokes.

"Did you know the ravens are supposed to protect the kingdom?" Ava asked, glancing at Emma. "If they ever leave, it's a sign of disaster."

"Good thing they're still here, then," Emma replied, though her attention was drawn to a group of guards near the Jewel House. They seemed to be arguing, their voices low but tense.

"...I swear, I saw something," one guard said, his tone insistent.

"And I'm telling you, there's no such thing," another replied, exasperation in his voice.

Emma frowned, nudging Leo. "Did you hear that?"

"Hear what?" Leo asked, glancing up from his phone.

"Those guards. They're talking about seeing something. Maybe a ghost?"

Leo raised an eyebrow. "Or maybe someone skipped breakfast. Come on, Em, let's not get carried away."

But Emma couldn't shake the feeling that something was off. She caught Sophie's eye and motioned subtly toward the guards. Sophie's grin widened; she lived for moments like this.

"Ghosts, huh?" Sophie said, sidling up to Emma. "Think it's real?"

"Probably not," Emma replied, though she wasn't entirely sure. "But it's worth keeping an eye on."

The group continued their exploration, moving from the outer walls to the more secure inner structures. Inside the White Tower, the displays of medieval weaponry and armour captivated Max, who eagerly rattled off details about each piece.

"This is a poleaxe," he said, pointing at a weapon taller than he was. "It was used in the 15th century, mostly for armoured combat."

"Cool," Leo said absentmindedly as he snapped a photo of an ancient sword.

Sophie, meanwhile, had drifted toward a display of the Tower's infamous prisoners. "Look at this," she said, gesturing to a plaque about Anne Boleyn. "Beheaded right here. Talk about a rough day."

"Can we not talk about beheadings?" Ava piped up, her voice tinged with nervousness.

"Sorry," Sophie said with a shrug. "But hey, if there are ghosts, she's probably one of them."

As they exited the White Tower and made their way toward the Jewel House, the atmosphere seemed to shift. The air felt heavier, colder, as though the shadows themselves were watching.

"Did anyone else feel that?" Sophie asked, rubbing her arms.

"Feel what?" Leo replied, but even he looked a little unsettled.

"The temperature dropped," Ava said quietly. "It's like someone turned on a freezer."

Emma glanced around, her instincts on high alert. "Let's stay close. I don't want anyone wandering off."

The Jewel House, where the Crown Jewels were displayed, was as dazzling as they'd expected. Ava's eyes widened as she took in the glittering crowns, sceptres, and ceremonial swords.

"They're even more beautiful in person," she whispered.

"Yeah, and heavily guarded," Leo added, pointing out the numerous security cameras and motion sensors.

Max, however, frowned as he read a nearby sign. "Something doesn't add up," he said.

"What do you mean?" Emma asked.

"It says here that all the jewels are accounted for, but I read an article last week about missing artifacts. Some of the lesser-known pieces disappeared a few months ago, and no one's found them yet."

"Maybe they don't want to panic the tourists," Leo suggested.

"Or maybe there's more to the story," Sophie said, her eyes gleaming. "Missing jewels, ghost sightings... sounds like a mystery to me."

Emma hesitated. As much as she hated getting distracted from their parents' instructions, she couldn't deny that the pieces were intriguing. If something strange was happening at the Tower, it wasn't just their curiosity—it was their responsibility to find out.

"Okay," she said finally. "Let's keep our ears open. If we hear or see anything unusual, we'll investigate. But no sneaking off alone."

"Deal," Sophie said with a mock salute.

As the siblings exited the Jewel House, the ravens cawed loudly from their perches, as if warning them. The shadows of the Tower stretched long across the ground, and Emma couldn't shake the feeling that their day was about to take a very unexpected turn.

What had started as a simple family trip was quickly becoming something else entirely. The Tower of London had secrets, and the Edmondsons were about to uncover them.

Chapter 2: Whispers in the Shadows

Ava's sketchbook rested on her lap as she sat on a low stone bench near the Tower Green, her pencil darting across the page. She had been working on a drawing of the Jewel House, trying to capture the way the light reflected off the ancient glass windows. The ravens cawed noisily overhead, but Ava found their presence comforting, like silent guardians of the Tower.

Her siblings had split off to explore other parts of the fortress, promising to meet back in half an hour. For once, Ava didn't mind being alone. She enjoyed the peace, the chance to focus on the tiny details she loved to capture in her sketches—the curve of a stone arch, the way the cobblestones seemed to tell their own stories.

She was so absorbed in her work that she almost didn't hear the voices nearby.

"...I'm telling you, it wasn't my imagination," a man said, his voice low and tense.

Ava froze, her pencil hovering over the page. She turned slightly, careful to keep herself hidden behind a large stone pillar.

"Keep your voice down," another man hissed. "Do you want to lose your job?"

"I don't care about the job right now," the first voice replied. "You didn't see what I saw. It was... it was like a figure, but not solid. Almost like smoke. It just floated there, near the Jewel House. And the sound—it wasn't human."

Ava's heart raced. She leaned forward slightly, straining to hear more.

"You've been working the night shifts too long," the second man said. "It's probably just shadows. The lights play tricks on your eyes, especially in a place like this."

"Shadows don't make sounds," the first man insisted. "And they don't disappear into walls."

There was a long pause before the second man spoke again, his voice quieter. "Even if you're right—and I'm not saying you are—you know we're not supposed to talk about it. You've heard the orders. Keep it quiet, or it'll be your head."

The first man let out a frustrated sigh. "Fine. But when something happens, don't say I didn't warn you."

Their footsteps echoed on the cobblestones as they walked away, leaving Ava alone with her thoughts. She sat perfectly still, her heart pounding. A ghostly figure? Strange sounds? And they were near the Jewel House?

She closed her sketchbook, her fingers trembling slightly. She needed to tell her siblings.

Ava found Emma and Sophie near the Beauchamp Tower, examining the carvings on the walls left by prisoners centuries ago. Max was nearby, his nose buried in his guidebook, while Leo fiddled with the settings on his camera.

"You guys," Ava said breathlessly, skidding to a stop in front of them. "I just heard something—something important."

Emma looked up from the inscription she'd been reading. "What is it, Ava?"

Ava glanced around, making sure no one else was close enough to overhear. "I was drawing by the Jewel House, and I heard two guards talking. One of them said he saw something—a figure, like smoke, floating near the jewels. And they heard a sound that wasn't human."

Max lowered his book, his brow furrowed. "Are you sure that's what they said?"

"I'm sure," Ava replied, her voice firm. "They sounded scared. And they mentioned being told not to talk about it."

Sophie's eyes lit up with excitement. "I knew it! Ghosts. This place has to be haunted."

Leo snorted. "Or they just saw a trick of the light. It's probably nothing."

"It doesn't sound like nothing," Emma said, her tone thoughtful. "If the guards are scared, there might be more to this than we realize. And if they've been told to keep quiet, that's even more suspicious."

"Exactly," Ava said, feeling vindicated. "We have to investigate."

Emma nodded. "We'll stick to the plan for now—gather as much information as we can without drawing attention to ourselves. If there's something going on, we'll figure it out."

That evening, as the sun dipped below the horizon and the Tower was bathed in a golden glow, the siblings regrouped near the walls overlooking the Thames. The day's tourists were leaving, and the atmosphere grew quieter, more solemn.

Max had spent the afternoon poring over old maps and plaques, while Leo had scoured the Tower's grounds for any sign of security anomalies. Sophie had been asking discreet questions of the staff, pretending to be a curious teenager with an interest in history.

"There's definitely a pattern," Max said, spreading out a photocopy of a map he'd found in the gift shop. "The Jewel House, the White Tower, and the Queen's House—all the sightings and strange sounds have been reported near these areas."

"That makes sense," Emma said. "Those are the oldest parts of the Tower. If there's any truth to the ghost stories, it would make sense for them to center there."

"But why would a ghost care about the jewels?" Sophie asked, leaning over the map.

"Maybe it doesn't," Max replied. "It could be tied to something else entirely. The Tower's history is full of tragedy and betrayal. Maybe the ghost is connected to one of those events."

"Or maybe it's not a ghost at all," Leo said, his tone sceptical. "It could be someone using the ghost story to cover up something else. Like stealing the Crown Jewels."

Ava's eyes widened. "You mean... like a distraction?"

"Exactly," Leo said. "If people are scared of ghosts, they're less likely to notice someone sneaking around."

Emma considered this. "It's possible. Either way, we need more information. Max, keep digging into the history of the Tower and see if there's anything that matches what the guards described. Leo, see if you can figure out how the security system works—without getting us caught. Sophie, Ava, and I will check out the Jewel House tonight."

"Wait," Max said, his expression concerned. "You're not planning to sneak in, are you?"

"Of course not," Emma said, though there was a mischievous glint in her eye. "We're just going to take a closer look."

As night fell, the Tower took on a completely different personality. The bustling crowds and cheerful chatter of the day were replaced by an eerie stillness. Shadows stretched long across the ancient stones, and the sound of the river seemed louder in the silence.

Emma, Sophie, and Ava approached the Jewel House, their footsteps muffled by the damp cobblestones. The building was dark, its imposing structure outlined by the faint glow of nearby lanterns.

"This is so creepy," Ava whispered, clutching her sketchbook tightly.

"I love it," Sophie whispered back, her grin barely visible in the dim light.

Emma motioned for them to be quiet as they crept closer. They stopped just short of the main entrance, staying hidden in the shadows.

For a moment, everything was still. Then Ava heard it—a faint, almost imperceptible sound, like a whisper carried on the wind.

"Did you hear that?" she whispered.

Emma and Sophie nodded, their eyes scanning the area. The sound came again, this time clearer—a low, mournful wail that seemed to echo from within the Jewel House.

Ava's heart pounded in her chest. She gripped Emma's arm tightly. "What is that?"

Before Emma could answer, a shadow flickered across one of the upper windows. It was faint, almost translucent, but unmistakable—a figure, cloaked in mist, moving through the darkness.

All three girls froze, their breath caught in their throats.

"Okay," Sophie whispered, her voice trembling slightly. "That was definitely not normal."

The shadow lingered for a moment longer before fading away, leaving the window empty once more.

Emma took a deep breath, forcing herself to stay calm. "We need to get back and tell the others. Now."

They hurried back to the meeting point, their footsteps quick and nervous. The Tower loomed behind them, its secrets pressing in from all sides.

Whatever they had just witnessed, one thing was clear: this was no ordinary mystery. And the Edmondsons were determined to solve it.

Chapter 3: A Ghostly Encounter

The Tower of London at night was a world apart from the lively, tourist-filled fortress it was during the day. The ancient stones seemed to hum with unspoken secrets, and the shadows stretched long and deep, swallowing everything they touched. It was the perfect setting for Sophie Edmondson, the fearless adventurer of the family, to satisfy her curiosity.

She couldn't sleep—not after what Ava had overheard earlier in the day, not after the strange sound and shadow they had witnessed near the Jewel House. Something was happening here, and Sophie couldn't stand waiting until morning to find out more.

Carefully, she slipped out of the small room she shared with Ava in the Tower's guest quarters, where their family was staying overnight as part of their parents' research arrangement. Quietly, she tiptoed down the corridor, past Leo and Max's door, and out into the cool night air.

The chill wrapped around her like a cloak as she stepped onto the cobblestones. The Tower loomed large and imposing, its darkened windows watching like empty eyes. Sophie grinned to herself. This was her kind of adventure.

The Tower grounds were eerily quiet as Sophie moved through the shadows. She had memorized the guard rotations earlier in the day—just in case—and knew she had a small window to explore undisturbed.

Her first stop was the Jewel House. She stayed just out of sight, peering at the building from behind a stone column. Nothing seemed out of place at first, but Sophie had learned to trust her instincts. Something was here; she could feel it.

Then she heard it.

A faint rustling sound, like fabric brushing against stone, reached her ears. It was soft but distinct, and it came from just beyond the Jewel House. Sophie froze, her breath caught in her throat.

The sound grew louder, closer. Slowly, she peeked around the column, her heart pounding.

There it was.

A figure, pale and glowing faintly in the darkness, glided across the courtyard. It was translucent, its edges shimmering like smoke caught in the moonlight. The figure's shape was indistinct, but it moved with purpose, as if searching for something.

Sophie's first instinct was to follow. She crept forward, staying low and quiet, her heart racing with both fear and excitement. The figure didn't seem to notice her, its attention fixed ahead as it floated toward the White Tower.

As it reached the base of the ancient structure, the figure paused. Sophie ducked behind a low wall, watching as the ghostly form seemed to study the stones. Its hand—or what passed for one—reached out, brushing against the wall. Then, as suddenly as it had appeared, the figure began to fade.

"No," Sophie whispered, barely aware she had spoken aloud.

She leaned forward, desperate to see more, but the figure was gone. The courtyard was silent once more, the chill in the air feeling sharper than before.

Sophie stayed crouched for a long moment, her mind racing. What had she just seen? It had to be a ghost—nothing else could explain the way it moved, the way it vanished. But why was it here? And what was it searching for?

By the time Sophie returned to the guest quarters, her hands were trembling. She wasn't scared—at least, not exactly—but she felt a new sense of urgency. The Tower's secrets were real, and whatever was happening here, they were now a part of it.

She slipped back into her room, careful not to wake Ava. But Ava, ever perceptive, stirred anyway.

"Sophie?" she mumbled sleepily, rubbing her eyes. "Where were you?"

Sophie hesitated, then whispered, "I saw it, Ava. The ghost. It's real."

Ava sat up instantly, her drowsiness forgotten. "You saw it? What did it look like? What happened?"

"I'll tell everyone in the morning," Sophie said, her voice steady despite the whirlwind of emotions inside her. "But we need to investigate. There's definitely something going on here, and I think the ghost is trying to show us something."

Ava nodded, her excitement mirroring Sophie's. "I knew it! We have to tell Emma and the others first thing."

Sophie nodded, already planning her next move. Tomorrow, they would put their heads together and figure out what to do. The ghost was a clue—a piece of a much larger puzzle—and Sophie was determined to solve it.

As she lay down, her thoughts raced with possibilities. The Tower of London had seen centuries of history, but it was about to witness something new: the Edmondson siblings, ready to uncover the truth.

Chapter 4: Unlikely Clues

The next morning, the siblings gathered in the common area of the guest quarters, their faces alight with excitement and anticipation. Sophie's recount of the ghostly figure had sparked a whirlwind of questions, theories, and plans, but it was Max who insisted they pause for a moment to regroup.

"Before we start running around looking for ghosts," Max said, adjusting his glasses, "I want to see if there's any historical basis for what Sophie saw. Ghost stories don't just appear out of thin air—there's usually some kind of origin."

"Great," Leo said with a smirk. "While you dig through dusty old books, the rest of us can handle the action."

"History is action," Max shot back, his cheeks flushing slightly. "Or at least it leads to it. Trust me on this."

Emma, always the voice of reason, stepped in. "Let's split up. Max, see what you can find in the Tower's library or archives. Leo, keep looking into the security systems—you might find something that connects to the ghost's appearances. Sophie, Ava, and I will retrace the ghost's path from last night and see if there are any physical clues."

"Divide and conquer," Sophie said with a grin. "Works for me."

Max made his way to the Tower's small research library, a tucked-away space filled with dusty tomes, old maps, and artifacts not yet on display. It was his favorite kind of place: quiet, filled with potential discoveries, and, most importantly, unassuming.

He settled into a corner desk with a stack of books and began flipping through their pages, searching for anything related to hauntings, hidden chambers, or the Crown Jewels. Most of the books contained the usual fare—legends about Anne Boleyn's ghost, accounts of imprisoned traitors, and vague mentions of curses.

Then, in a worn, leather-bound book that seemed far older than the others, Max found something intriguing. The title, Tales of the Tower:

Lost Legends and Forgotten Secrets, immediately caught his attention. He opened it carefully, the pages crackling with age.

One chapter in particular stood out: The Shadowed Vaults of the Jewel House.

Max's pulse quickened as he read. The passage described an old legend about a hidden chamber beneath the Tower, said to house treasures from long-forgotten eras. According to the account, the chamber was protected by both physical barriers and a supernatural guardian—a spirit that appeared as a figure of mist and shadow.

"It's here!" Max muttered to himself, his eyes scanning the text.

The book detailed sightings similar to Sophie's description: a ghostly figure appearing near the Jewel House and the White Tower, moving as if searching for something. The account claimed that the spirit was not malevolent but acted as a protector, warning of danger to the Crown Jewels and guarding the secret of the hidden chamber.

Max leaned back in his chair, his mind racing. Could this hidden chamber still exist? And if it did, was it somehow tied to the recent thefts and ghost sightings?

By the time Max rejoined the group in the afternoon, he was practically vibrating with excitement.

"You won't believe what I found," he said, dropping the book onto the table in front of them.

Emma picked it up, flipping through the pages. "What is it?"

"A historical account of the Tower's hauntings," Max explained. "It mentions a hidden chamber beneath the Jewel House. According to legend, the chamber holds treasures that were hidden centuries ago—and it's guarded by a ghostly figure that sounds exactly like what Sophie saw."

Sophie leaned in, her eyes wide. "Are you serious? The ghost is protecting a secret chamber?"

"That's what it says," Max replied. "And it gets better. The chamber is supposed to be hidden behind a section of wall that's been sealed for hundreds of years. The only way to open it is to find a specific set of symbols carved into the stone."

"Symbols?" Ava asked, already pulling out her sketchbook. "Like what?"

"I don't know," Max admitted. "The book didn't describe them in detail. But it did say they're small and easy to miss. If the ghost is showing up near the Jewel House, the entrance to the chamber might be close by."

Emma tapped her chin thoughtfully. "This could explain a lot. If someone was trying to break into the hidden chamber, they might use the ghost stories as a distraction—or even try to manipulate the legend for their own purposes."

"Or maybe the ghost is trying to warn us," Ava added.

Leo, who had been listening quietly, finally spoke. "It's an interesting theory, but we're still missing a lot of pieces. If we're going to find this chamber—and figure out what's really going on—we'll need to be smart about it. No running in blind."

"Agreed," Emma said. "Max, great work finding this. Let's focus on two things: figuring out where the hidden chamber might be and seeing if the ghost shows up again tonight. We'll split into two teams—one to investigate the area near the Jewel House, and one to keep an eye on the White Tower."

Sophie grinned. "Finally, some action."

As the siblings began to plan their next steps, the weight of the mystery settled over them. The Tower of London was full of secrets, but they were determined to uncover the truth. A ghost, a hidden chamber, and stolen Crown Jewels—this was shaping up to be their greatest adventure yet.

Chapter 5: Tech Trouble

Leo sat cross-legged on the floor of the Edmondsons' guest quarters, his laptop balanced on his knees and a tangle of cables spilling out of his backpack. The rest of the siblings hovered nearby, watching as he worked.

"If we're going to figure out what's really happening," he said, typing rapidly, "we need eyes on the ground—or in this case, on the security feeds. The Tower must have cameras all over the place. If the ghost shows up, we should be able to spot it."

"Do you think it'll work?" Ava asked, leaning over his shoulder.

"Shouldn't be too hard," Leo replied, smirking. "Most security systems have weak spots, and once I'm in, we can access a live feed of the whole area. If anything weird happens, we'll catch it."

Emma crossed her arms, her brow furrowed. "Just don't trip any alarms. The last thing we need is for the Tower staff to catch us hacking into their system."

"I'm not a total amateur," Leo said, rolling his eyes. "Trust me, they'll never know we were here."

After an hour of carefully navigating the Tower's network, Leo finally managed to break into the surveillance system. Multiple camera feeds appeared on his screen, each one displaying a different section of the Tower.

"There we go," he said, grinning triumphantly. "Now we're in business."

The siblings crowded around the laptop, watching the feeds flicker between various locations: the Jewel House, the White Tower, the Tower Green, and several shadowy corridors. Everything seemed normal at first—guards patrolling, a raven fluttering across the courtyard, the faint glow of the moon casting long shadows over the ancient stones.

"Wait," Sophie said, pointing at the screen. "Go back to the Jewel House."

Leo rewound the footage, his fingers flying across the keyboard. The camera angle showed the Jewel House entrance, bathed in dim light. For a moment, nothing seemed out of the ordinary. Then, a strange distortion rippled across the screen, like a glitch in the footage.

"What was that?" Max asked, leaning closer.

"I don't know," Leo muttered, rewinding the footage again. "It's like the camera glitched, but it's only happening here. Look—none of the other feeds are affected."

As they watched, the distortion happened again. This time, it was accompanied by a faint flickering of light near the Jewel House entrance, almost like a shadow passing in front of the camera.

"That's not normal," Emma said, her tone sharp. "Is it happening in real-time, or just on the recorded footage?"

"Let me check," Leo replied, switching to the live feed. He stared at the screen, his fingers hovering over the keyboard. At first, everything seemed fine. Then, without warning, the screen went black.

"What happened?" Ava asked, her voice rising with alarm.

"The feed just... cut out," Leo said, frowning. He switched to another camera, but it was also offline. One by one, the feeds began to blink out, until the entire system was down.

"This isn't me," Leo said, his voice tense. "Something's interfering with the cameras."

"Interfering how?" Sophie asked.

"Could be electrical," Leo said, shaking his head. "Or something... else."

Max, ever the logical one, chimed in. "The ghost."

Leo gave him a sceptical look. "You think a ghost is messing with the surveillance system?"

"Why not?" Max replied. "If the ghost is tied to the Tower's history, maybe it doesn't want to be watched. Or maybe it's trying to keep something hidden."

"Either way, it's a problem," Emma said. "Without the cameras, we're blind. Can you get the system back online?"

"I can try," Leo said, already typing again. "But this kind of blackout doesn't just happen. Someone—or something—is doing this on purpose."

After another thirty minutes of troubleshooting, Leo managed to restore a few of the feeds, but the ones closest to the Jewel House and the White Tower remained offline.

"It's like there's a dead zone," he explained, frustrated. "Whatever's causing this, it's centered around the areas where the ghost has been seen. And it's not just the cameras—it's the motion sensors, too. They're not registering anything."

Emma frowned, pacing the room. "If the cameras and sensors are failing, that leaves the Tower vulnerable. If someone wanted to steal something—or break into the hidden chamber Max found—this would be the perfect cover."

"Exactly," Leo said. "Whoever—or whatever—is behind this knows what they're doing."

Sophie, who had been unusually quiet, finally spoke. "Then we need to go back out there. Tonight. If the cameras can't see what's happening, we'll have to see for ourselves."

Emma hesitated, glancing at the others. She didn't like the idea of sneaking around again, especially with so many unknowns, but Sophie was right. If they wanted answers, they couldn't rely on the technology alone.

"Okay," Emma said finally. "We'll split into pairs. Leo, stay here and monitor the feeds in case they come back online. The rest of us will check the Jewel House and the White Tower. If anything happens, we'll signal each other."

As the siblings prepared for their nighttime investigation, the atmosphere in the Tower grew heavier. The shadows seemed darker, the air colder, and the ancient stones whispered secrets they couldn't quite hear.

Leo stayed behind, watching the flickering screens and trying to make sense of the strange anomalies. But even as he worked, he couldn't shake the feeling that something—or someone—was watching them, just beyond the reach of the cameras.

Whatever was haunting the Tower, it wasn't finished yet. And neither were the Edmondsons.

Chapter 6: The Ghost's Warning

The Tower of London was cloaked in silence, its ancient stones bathed in the pale glow of the moon. Emma, Sophie, Max, and Ava crept through the Jewel House courtyard, their footsteps muffled by the damp cobblestones. The previous night's events—the ghostly figure Sophie had seen and the strange anomalies Leo had uncovered—had left them on edge. Tonight, they were determined to get answers.

"Everyone stay close," Emma whispered, her voice barely audible. "If we see anything unusual, don't engage. We need to observe and figure out what's going on."

The siblings moved cautiously, their senses heightened. Max carried a small notebook, ready to jot down any clues, while Sophie and Ava kept their eyes peeled for movement in the shadows. Emma held a flashlight, its beam cutting through the darkness like a thin blade.

As they approached the Jewel House, a faint, icy breeze swirled around them, carrying with it the unmistakable feeling of being watched. Sophie stopped suddenly, her hand shooting out to grab Emma's arm.

"There!" she whispered, pointing toward the base of the White Tower.

The others followed her gaze. A faint, glowing figure hovered near the wall, its translucent form shimmering like mist in the moonlight. It moved slowly, almost deliberately, as if searching for something.

"That's it," Sophie breathed. "That's the ghost I saw."

The figure paused, its hazy hand reaching toward the stone wall. As the siblings watched in tense silence, the ghost began to move its fingers, tracing something into the air—a series of shapes and lines that glowed faintly before fading away.

"Max, write that down," Emma said urgently.

Max scrambled to copy the shapes into his notebook, his hands trembling slightly. "It looks like... symbols," he muttered. "They're not random."

Before he could finish, the ghost turned suddenly, its glowing form flickering as if caught in a gust of wind. It raised an arm, pointing directly at the siblings. Ava gasped, clutching Sophie's sleeve, but the ghost didn't move closer. Instead, it began to fade, its outline dissolving into the night.

The siblings stood frozen, the weight of what they'd just witnessed settling over them.

"What was it pointing at?" Ava asked, her voice barely a whisper.

"I don't know," Emma said, her brow furrowed. "But whatever it was, it wanted us to notice."

Back in their quarters, the siblings gathered around Max's notebook, poring over the symbols he had copied. The shapes were rough but distinct: a series of interlocking lines, circles, and angles that seemed almost like an ancient script.

"It's not any language I recognize," Emma said, frowning. "Max?"

Max flipped through his guidebook, searching for anything similar. "It's not Latin, or Old English, or anything else from this region. But it could be a cipher."

Leo, who had just returned from monitoring the surveillance feeds, leaned over the notebook. "A cipher? Like a code?"

"Exactly," Max said, his excitement building. "If the ghost is trying to tell us something, it would make sense to use a code. Maybe it thought we'd understand."

"Or maybe it's just trying to confuse us," Sophie said, though her curiosity was clear. "Do you think you can crack it?"

Max nodded, already grabbing a pencil. "It might take some time, but I'll give it a shot."

Hours later, as the others dozed off, Max finally sat up straight, his face alight with discovery. "I think I've got it!"

The siblings gathered around him, their exhaustion forgotten.

"The symbols are a substitution cipher," Max explained, pointing to his notes. "Once I matched each symbol to a letter, I got this message: 'Betrayed within. Treasure stolen. Seek the hidden truth.'"

"'Betrayed within'?" Emma repeated, her voice tense. "That sounds like someone on the inside. Maybe a guard or staff member?"

"'Treasure stolen' is pretty obvious," Leo said. "It's talking about the missing jewels."

"But what's 'seek the hidden truth' supposed to mean?" Ava asked.

Emma's eyes narrowed as she considered the possibilities. "It could mean the hidden chamber Max found in that old book. If the ghost is connected to the chamber, it might be trying to lead us there."

"Then we need to find it," Sophie said firmly. "The ghost is clearly trying to help us. And if someone really has betrayed the Tower, we might be the only ones who can figure out who it is."

The siblings spent the rest of the night planning their next move. Armed with the ghost's cryptic warning and the knowledge of a possible hidden chamber, they knew they were on the brink of uncovering something huge. But with every step forward, the stakes grew higher. Whoever—or whatever—was behind the Tower's mysteries wouldn't give up their secrets without a fight.

As the first rays of dawn broke over the Tower of London, the Edmondsons prepared themselves for the next phase of their investigation. The ghost's warning was clear: betrayal and theft were at the heart of the mystery, and the truth was hidden somewhere deep within the ancient walls.

The game was on.

Chapter 7: Hidden Histories

The Tower of London's library was a treasure trove of forgotten stories and half-buried truths. Max Edmondson, the family's resident history buff, had spent the morning scouring shelves lined with leather-bound tomes, yellowing manuscripts, and ancient scrolls. His siblings had given him the task of finding any connection between the Tower's ghostly warnings, the stolen jewels, and the cryptic message they had deciphered the night before.

His persistence finally paid off when he stumbled upon an old, battered book titled The Tower's Forgotten Treasures. Its faded cover bore an emblem of a crown encircled by a serpent, an image that sent a thrill of curiosity through him.

Max carefully flipped through the fragile pages until a chapter caught his attention: The Curse of the Raven's Heart.

The chapter detailed a legend dating back to the late 14th century. According to the text, the Raven's Heart was a magnificent jewel, deep red and as large as a man's fist. It was said to have been commissioned by King Richard II, who believed it would secure his reign and protect the Tower from enemies.

But the jewel's beauty came at a cost. The craftsman who created it—a mysterious alchemist named Elias Ravenscroft—was rumoured to have cursed it. Ravenscroft had been betrayed by the king's advisors, who imprisoned him within the Tower and ordered his execution once the jewel was completed. In his final moments, the legend claimed, Ravenscroft uttered a chilling warning:

"The Raven's Heart will protect no master who betrays its maker. It will guard the Tower, but only in loyalty. Betrayal will bring ruin, and the jewel will vanish, leaving only shadows in its wake."

The jewel was said to have disappeared shortly after Richard II's reign ended in turmoil. Over the centuries, there were scattered reports of the Raven's Heart being sighted or referenced in secret documents, but no one had ever found it. Some believed it was hidden within the Tower itself, while others thought it had been taken by a traitor and lost to history.

Max's pulse quickened as he read. The parallels were too strong to ignore. The cryptic message from the ghost spoke of betrayal and theft—exactly what Ravenscroft had warned about.

"What if the Raven's Heart is real?" Max murmured to himself. "And what if someone's trying to find it—or already has?"

Max hurried back to the guest quarters, the book tucked under his arm. He found his siblings gathered around a table strewn with notes, maps, and Leo's laptop.

"Guys, you're not going to believe this," Max said, dropping the book onto the table and flipping to the chapter on the Raven's Heart.

"What is it?" Emma asked, leaning over to read.

Max quickly summarized the legend, his excitement spilling over as he explained the curse and the jewel's mysterious disappearance.

"Wait," Sophie said, her eyes wide. "You're saying the ghost might be connected to this cursed jewel?"

"It makes sense," Max said, nodding. "The ghost warned us about betrayal and theft, and the Raven's Heart is all about loyalty and punishment for betrayal. If the jewel is hidden somewhere in the Tower, it could explain why the ghost is appearing now. Maybe someone's trying to steal it—or maybe the curse is already at work."

"What if the stolen Crown Jewels were a distraction?" Ava suggested. "To keep people from noticing that someone's looking for the Raven's Heart?"

"That would explain the anomalies with the cameras and motion sensors," Leo added. "If someone's been sneaking around the Tower trying to find this thing, they'd want to keep it under the radar."

Emma paced the room, her mind racing. "If the Raven's Heart is real, it's not just a jewel—it's a weapon. If someone gets their hands on it, who knows what they could do? We need to find it before they do."

The siblings decided to divide their efforts. Max would continue researching the legend, looking for clues about the jewel's possible location. Emma, Sophie, and Ava would search the areas where the ghost had appeared, keeping an eye out for any carvings or symbols that matched the ones described in the legend. Leo would monitor the surveillance feeds and investigate the technical glitches.

As they prepared to set out, Max couldn't shake the feeling that they were on the verge of something monumental. The Tower of London was a place steeped in history, but this mystery felt personal, as if the Tower itself were calling to them.

Later that evening, Max made a breakthrough. Hidden in the back of the same book, he found a crude map of the Tower, marked with a symbol he recognized: the same crown encircled by a serpent that had been on the book's cover. The map pointed to a location near the base of the White Tower, a spot that had been sealed off for centuries.

"Look at this," Max said, showing the map to Emma and the others. "If the Raven's Heart is anywhere, it's here. And it lines up with where the ghost has been appearing."

"Then that's where we're going," Emma said, her voice firm.

"But we need to be careful," Max added. "If the curse is real—and the ghost is tied to it—we don't know what we're walking into."

Emma nodded, her expression serious. "We'll be ready. Whatever's waiting for us, we're not backing down."

The Raven's Heart, the ghost, the stolen jewels—it was all connected. And now, the siblings were closer than ever to uncovering the Tower's darkest secret.

Chapter 8: The Ravenkeeper's Tale

The following morning, the siblings made their way to the Tower Green, where the ravens perched in their usual spots along the battlements and stone walls. Their black feathers gleamed in the soft light of the overcast sky, their sharp eyes following the movements of every visitor.

"I read that the ravens are supposed to protect the Tower," Ava said, craning her neck to get a better look at one particularly large bird. "If they ever leave, it's supposed to mean the kingdom will fall."

"Well, they're still here," Leo said with a smirk. "Guess we're safe—for now."

Max was flipping through his notes. "The legend of the Raven's Heart mentioned the ravens too. Ravenscroft, the alchemist who made the jewel, might have named it after them. They could be part of the curse."

"Or they just like shiny things," Sophie said, watching one raven peck at a discarded coin.

Their conversation was interrupted by the arrival of an older man in a dark coat, carrying a small satchel of food scraps. His weathered face broke into a curious smile as he noticed the siblings.

"You've got an interest in the ravens, eh?" he said in a deep, gravelly voice.

"Are you the Ravenkeeper?" Emma asked, stepping forward.

"That I am," the man replied with a nod. "Name's Alistair. Been looking after these beauties for twenty-five years."

The siblings exchanged excited glances. If anyone knew the Tower's secrets, it was this man.

Alistair led them to a quieter corner of the courtyard, away from the bustle of tourists. He pulled a few scraps of meat from his satchel and tossed them to the nearest raven, which cawed appreciatively.

"You lot seem different from the usual visitors," he said, his sharp eyes studying them. "Not just here for the history, are you?"

"We're… curious about some of the stories," Emma said cautiously. "Particularly the ghost sightings."

Alistair's face darkened. He glanced around to ensure they were alone before lowering his voice. "So you've heard, then."

"We've seen it," Sophie said. "Or at least, I have. A ghostly figure near the White Tower."

Alistair let out a long sigh. "I was hoping it wasn't true, but the ravens have been acting strange. It's always a sign."

"What do you mean?" Max asked, leaning forward.

Alistair gestured to the ravens perched nearby. "These birds are more than just symbols—they're watchers. They see what others miss. And when they start acting up, it means something's wrong."

"Acting up how?" Ava asked.

"Flying at odd hours, refusing to return to their roosts, cawing in the middle of the night," Alistair said. "And it's not just one or two of them—it's the whole lot. Last week, I found three of them clustered around the Jewel House at midnight, staring at the door like they were guarding it. And the night before that, one flew straight into the White Tower window, as if trying to get inside."

"That's not normal," Max said, scribbling furiously in his notebook.

"No, it's not," Alistair said, his voice grim. "The last time they acted like this was years ago, when the Crown Jewels were nearly stolen. It's as if they sense danger before we do. But this time… it feels different. Darker."

"Do you think it has to do with the ghost?" Emma asked.

Alistair nodded slowly. "If what you saw is real, then yes. The ghost and the ravens are connected somehow. And if the stories about the Raven's Heart are true, it's no coincidence. That jewel was cursed to protect the Tower, and the ravens are part of its watch."

The siblings exchanged uneasy glances. Everything was starting to fall into place: the ghostly warnings, the anomalies around the Jewel House, the legends of the cursed jewel.

"Is there anything else you've noticed?" Emma asked. "Anything that might help us figure out what's going on?"

Alistair hesitated, then reached into his satchel and pulled out a small, gleaming object. It was a fragment of red glass, jagged and translucent, with a faint, eerie glow.

"I found this near the Jewel House a few nights ago," he said, handing it to Max. "It's not part of the Crown Jewels—I'd recognize it if it were. But it feels... wrong."

Max held the fragment up to the light, his brow furrowing. "It's not just glass. It could be part of something larger—maybe even the Raven's Heart."

The siblings fell silent, the weight of the discovery sinking in. If the fragment was part of the Raven's Heart, then the jewel wasn't just a legend. It was real—and it was already breaking apart.

As they thanked Alistair and made their way back to their quarters, Emma turned to the group.

"We have to find the rest of the Raven's Heart," she said firmly. "If it's tied to the Tower's curse, it could explain everything—the ghost, the strange behaviour, even the missing jewels. And if someone else is looking for it, we need to stop them before they get to it first."

The siblings nodded in agreement, their determination renewed. The Tower of London's ravens had sounded the alarm, and the Edmondsons were ready to answer the call.

Chapter 9: Locked Doors and Secrets

Emma led the siblings along the shadowed path near the White Tower, her sharp eyes scanning every detail of the fortress. The conversation with Alistair, the Ravenkeeper, had left them more determined than ever to uncover the truth. The fragment of the Raven's Heart in Max's possession was proof that the ancient legend wasn't just a story. But it raised even more questions—where was the rest of the jewel, and who was trying to find it?

"If the Raven's Heart is real, it's got to be hidden somewhere deep in the Tower," Max said, his voice hushed. "The restricted areas are our best bet."

"And also the hardest places to get into," Leo pointed out. "We're talking high security—guards, cameras, and who knows what else."

"Nothing's impossible," Sophie said with a grin. "We just have to figure out how to get past them."

Emma, as always, stayed focused. "Let's scout the area first. We're not breaking any rules unless we have to."

The siblings had learned that one of the Tower's restricted sections was located in the lower levels of the White Tower—a labyrinth of old storage rooms, vaults, and sealed chambers. They made their way to the Tower's entrance, blending in with the lingering tourists. As they descended the stone stairs into the cooler, dimly lit interior, the air seemed heavier, charged with a sense of history—and secrecy.

Emma noticed a heavy wooden door at the far end of a corridor. A small sign hung on it: Restricted Access: Authorized Personnel Only. Two guards stood nearby, their post unyielding. Emma stopped the group a safe distance away and studied the scene.

"That has to be it," Emma whispered. "If there's something worth hiding, it's behind that door."

"Any chance they're guarding a stash of snacks instead of cursed jewels?" Leo quipped.

"Not likely," Max said, adjusting his glasses. "Based on the map I found yesterday, that door leads to rooms that haven't been used in centuries. If the Raven's Heart is anywhere, it could be there."

"So how do we get past them?" Sophie asked, her eyes gleaming with excitement.

Emma frowned, considering their options. "We're not going to get through with brute force or sneaking past—it's too risky. We need a distraction."

The siblings huddled together, brainstorming. After a few minutes, Leo smirked. "I've got just the thing."

From his backpack, he pulled out a small device—a gadget he'd been working on for months. "This baby can create a temporary audio distraction. I'll place it near the guards, set it off, and they'll think there's something happening down the hall. We'll have a short window to check out the door."

"Won't they come back as soon as they figure out it's nothing?" Ava asked.

"That's why we work fast," Emma said. "Sophie, you're with me. Max, you and Ava keep watch. Leo, you handle the distraction."

Once the plan was set, Leo crept to a spot near the guards and placed his gadget behind a low stone wall. With a quick tap on his phone, he activated the device. A loud, echoing clatter erupted, sounding like metal crashing against stone.

The guards stiffened immediately, their hands moving to their radios. One gestured toward the noise, and the other nodded.

"Let's check it out," one said, and they hurried down the hall, disappearing around a corner.

"Now!" Emma whispered, and she and Sophie dashed toward the restricted door.

The door was solid oak reinforced with iron, and a keypad was mounted on the wall beside it. Emma examined it quickly. "Looks like a simple passcode lock. Leo?"

"On it," Leo said, jogging over and pulling out another small device. He connected it to the keypad, and within seconds, the lock clicked open.

"Nice work," Sophie said as Emma pushed the door open.

Inside, the room was dimly lit, with narrow shelves and dusty crates piled high. The air was stale, and cobwebs hung from the low ceiling. It looked like the room hadn't been touched in years.

Emma moved quickly, her flashlight cutting through the darkness. "Look for anything out of place—markings, carvings, anything that might connect to the Raven's Heart."

Sophie scanned the shelves, running her fingers along the edges of old wooden boxes. "Most of this stuff looks like junk. Rusty tools, broken bits of armour... wait—what's this?"

She pulled out a small metal chest, its lid engraved with the same serpent-and-crown emblem they had seen in Max's book. Emma joined her, running her fingers over the intricate design.

"This is it," Emma said. "It has to be connected to the Raven's Heart."

"Can you open it?" Sophie asked.

Emma tried the latch, but it was locked tight. "Not here. We need to get this out before the guards come back."

As they hurried back toward the door, Max appeared in the doorway, signalling frantically. "The guards are coming back!"

Leo cursed under his breath. "We need to go—now!"

Emma and Sophie moved quickly, carrying the chest between them as they slipped out of the room. Leo shut the door behind them, locking it just as the guards returned to their post.

The siblings ducked behind a nearby alcove, holding their breath as the guards resumed their positions. After a tense moment, Emma motioned for them to retreat.

"Let's get back to the quarters," she whispered. "We'll figure out what's inside this chest there."

Back in their room, the siblings examined the chest more closely. It was old but well-preserved, its lock worn but sturdy.

"Stand back," Leo said, pulling out a small toolkit. Within moments, he had the lock open with a satisfying click.

The lid creaked as Emma lifted it, revealing a single item inside: a weathered piece of parchment. The edges were brittle, but the writing was still legible—a series of symbols similar to those the ghost had traced in the air.

"What does it say?" Ava asked, peering over Emma's shoulder.

Max studied the symbols, his brow furrowed. "It's a map. And I think it's pointing to the hidden chamber."

Emma's heart raced. They were one step closer to finding the Raven's Heart—and to uncovering the truth about the Tower's curse. But as the siblings stared at the map, a heavy silence fell over the room.

If the legend was real, what dangers awaited them in the chamber?

Emma closed the chest and looked at her siblings. "This is it. We're getting closer. But whatever happens next, we stick together. Agreed?"

"Agreed," they said in unison.

The Tower's secrets were within reach, but the hardest part of their journey was just beginning.

Chapter 10: Ava's Sketch

The siblings sat clustered around the small wooden table in their quarters, their latest discovery—the weathered map from the chest—spread out before them. The ancient parchment's symbols were faint, its edges worn, but Max had done his best to trace the markings onto a fresh piece of paper for easier interpretation.

"It's definitely pointing somewhere," Max said, running his fingers along the lines. "But it's hard to tell exactly where. The markings are too vague."

"What about the ghost?" Ava asked, her voice thoughtful. "Remember how it drew those glowing symbols in the air? Maybe they're connected to the ones on the map."

Emma nodded. "Good point. Did anyone get a clear look at them?"

"I tried," Max admitted, looking frustrated. "But it all happened so fast. I didn't get a chance to write them down."

"I think I can help," Ava said, setting her sketchbook on the table.

Sophie raised an eyebrow. "How? You didn't even see the symbols that clearly."

"No," Ava said, flipping through her notebook, "but I remember the way they looked. I can picture them perfectly in my head."

"You think you can draw them?" Emma asked, her voice tinged with hope.

Ava nodded, pulling out her pencil. "Just give me a minute."

The room fell silent as Ava worked, her pencil gliding across the paper with practiced precision. Her photographic memory was one of her greatest strengths—she could recall even the smallest details of something she'd only glimpsed briefly.

The others watched in awe as the faint outline of the ghostly symbols began to take shape. Circles and intersecting lines emerged, intricate and almost mesmerizing in their complexity. Ava paused, her brow furrowed as she added the finishing touches.

"Done," she said, pushing the sketch toward Max.

He studied it closely, comparing it to the map. "This... this is incredible, Ava. It's almost an exact match. Look—this symbol here," he said, pointing to a looping figure, "is the same as the one on the map. It might be a key to figuring out where the chamber is."

Emma leaned over the table, her eyes narrowing as she examined the sketch. "If the ghost was trying to communicate with us, this symbol could be the clue we need to unlock the next part of the puzzle."

"But what does it mean?" Sophie asked. "It's not like we can just walk up to a wall and say, 'Open sesame.'"

Max flipped through his notes, his excitement building. "Wait a minute—this symbol reminds me of something I read in the legend of the Raven's Heart. The alchemist who made the jewel, Elias Ravenscroft, supposedly used a series of runes to seal the chamber. This could be one of them!"

"So if we find this symbol somewhere in the Tower..." Emma began.

"It might lead us to the chamber," Max finished.

The siblings decided to split up and search the areas of the Tower where the ghost had been seen. Armed with Ava's sketch and the map, they combed the Jewel House, the White Tower, and the surrounding courtyards, their eyes scanning every stone for a hint of the mysterious symbol.

It was Ava who spotted it first.

"Over here!" she called, her voice echoing slightly as she stood near the base of the White Tower.

The others rushed to her side, their breath catching as they saw what she was pointing at. Carved into the stone wall, nearly hidden beneath centuries of grime, was the exact symbol Ava had drawn.

"It's the same," Max said, his voice trembling with excitement.

"What now?" Sophie asked, running her fingers over the carving.

"There's got to be a mechanism," Leo said, already inspecting the area. "A hidden latch or a pressure point. These old chambers always have something like that."

Ava stepped back, her eyes scanning the wall with the same focus she used for her sketches. "Wait... there's another symbol, just below it."

Sure enough, a smaller marking was etched into the stone, almost invisible in the dim light. Max crouched down to study it, flipping through his notes.

"This one's different," he said. "It might be part of a sequence. Maybe we have to activate them in a certain order."

Emma stepped forward, her jaw set with determination. "Let's figure it out. Ava, you've already gotten us this far—what do you think?"

Ava hesitated, then pointed to the smaller symbol. "If this is part of a sequence, we should start here. It's positioned lower, almost like it's meant to be the beginning."

Emma nodded. "Let's try it."

Max pressed the smaller symbol, and a soft grinding noise echoed from within the wall. The siblings froze, holding their breath as a section of the stone shifted slightly, revealing a narrow gap.

"You did it!" Sophie whispered, her voice filled with awe.

Ava grinned, her excitement barely contained. "We did it."

The opening revealed a dark passageway, its interior lined with ancient stones slick with dampness. A faint, musty smell wafted out, and the air felt noticeably colder.

"Looks like we found the way in," Emma said, her voice steady despite the thrill of discovery coursing through her.

"But what's waiting for us in there?" Leo asked, peering into the shadows.

"Only one way to find out," Sophie said, stepping forward.

Emma held up a hand, stopping her. "Not yet. Let's get some supplies first—flashlights, ropes, anything we might need. We're not going in unprepared."

The siblings nodded, already buzzing with anticipation. The ghost's message, Ava's sketch, and the hidden symbol had led them to the threshold of the Tower's greatest secret.

Whatever lay beyond that passage, they were ready to face it—together.

Chapter 11: A Nighttime Stakeout

The Tower of London was eerily quiet at night, the bustling energy of the daytime crowds replaced by an oppressive stillness. The air was cold, the kind of damp chill that seemed to seep through clothing and settle into the bones. It was the perfect setting for a secret stakeout, and Sophie and Leo were ready for the challenge.

Armed with flashlights, a pair of binoculars, and Leo's custom tech gadgets, the siblings crouched in the shadows of a low stone wall near the Jewel House. From their vantage point, they had a clear view of the building's entrance and the surrounding area.

"This is either going to be really boring or really interesting," Sophie whispered, adjusting the hood of her jacket.

"I'm hoping for interesting," Leo replied, his fingers hovering over the keyboard of his laptop. He had set up a portable antenna to try to tap into the Tower's security system again, though he was still wary after the strange glitches from before.

"Do you think the ghost will show up?" Sophie asked, scanning the area with her binoculars.

"Maybe," Leo said. "But I'm more interested in finding out why the cameras keep blacking out. That's not normal, and I'm betting it's not the ghost."

The first hour passed uneventfully, with nothing but the occasional rustle of leaves and the distant sound of ravens cawing. Sophie was starting to fidget when Leo suddenly sat up straighter, his eyes fixed on his laptop screen.

"There's a signal spike," he whispered.

"What does that mean?" Sophie asked, leaning closer.

"It means someone's accessing the security system right now," Leo replied, his voice low but urgent. "But it's not coming from the Tower's main control room—it's coming from somewhere closer."

Sophie's pulse quickened. "Like... here?"

"Exactly," Leo said. "Whoever it is, they're not supposed to be doing this."

Sophie raised her binoculars again, sweeping the area. At first, she didn't see anything unusual. Then, near the far corner of the Jewel House, she spotted a faint movement.

"There," she whispered, nudging Leo. "Someone's by the side door."

Leo followed her gaze and squinted into the darkness. A shadowy figure was crouched near the wall, their movements deliberate and methodical.

"They're messing with something," Sophie said. "Probably the security panel."

Leo quickly tapped a few keys on his laptop, pulling up the limited feed he had managed to restore. The screen showed the side entrance to the Jewel House, but the image flickered and distorted.

"Whoever they are, they're causing the glitches," Leo said. "I can't get a clear view."

"Let's get closer," Sophie said, already moving.

The siblings crept toward the side of the Jewel House, staying low and sticking to the shadows. As they approached, the faint hum of electronics grew louder.

The figure was dressed in black, their face obscured by a hood. They were tinkering with a small device attached to the security panel, a faint blue light illuminating their gloved hands.

"What are they doing?" Sophie whispered.

"Looks like they're bypassing the system," Leo replied. "If they succeed, they'll have access to the Crown Jewels—or anything else inside."

"We have to stop them," Sophie said, her hand tightening on her flashlight.

"Not yet," Leo said, grabbing her arm. "We need evidence first. If we confront them now, they might escape, and we'll lose our chance to prove anything."

Sophie nodded reluctantly, and they stayed hidden, watching as the figure worked. After a few tense minutes, the person stood up, slipping the device into their pocket and glancing around.

"They're leaving," Leo whispered.

"Follow them?" Sophie asked.

Leo hesitated. "We should, but let's be smart about it. Keep your distance."

The siblings trailed the figure as they moved through the Tower grounds, careful to stay out of sight. The person seemed to know the area well, taking a circuitous route to avoid detection.

Finally, they disappeared into a small side building near the outer wall, one that appeared to be a maintenance shed.

"Why would they go in there?" Sophie asked.

"Good question," Leo said. "Let's check it out—but carefully."

The door to the shed was slightly ajar, and Sophie peered inside, her heart racing. The room was cluttered with tools and storage boxes, but what caught her attention was the laptop set up on a workbench.

Leo stepped inside, his eyes widening as he saw the screen. "They've got access to the entire security network," he said, pointing to the live feeds displayed on the monitor. "They've been monitoring the cameras and disabling the ones near the Jewel House."

Sophie spotted something else: a notebook lying open beside the laptop. She picked it up, flipping through the pages. It was filled with diagrams of the Tower, notes about guard rotations, and sketches of the Jewel House's interior.

"They've been planning this for a while," Sophie said.

"We need to tell Emma," Leo said, pulling out his phone. "And we need to get out of here before they come back."

Back in their quarters, Sophie and Leo relayed everything to the rest of the team.

"Whoever it is, they're not just looking for the Crown Jewels," Leo said. "They're trying to get into the restricted areas too. This is bigger than we thought."

"And more dangerous," Emma said, her expression grim. "If they're tampering with the security system, they could have access to anything—or anyone—inside the Tower."

"We need to figure out who they are," Max said, "and what they're really after."

Sophie set the notebook on the table. "This might help. Whoever they are, they've got a map of the restricted areas, and they've been focusing on the same places the ghost has appeared."

Emma studied the pages, her jaw tightening. "If they're looking for the Raven's Heart, we can't let them find it first. We're going to have to step up our game."

The siblings exchanged determined glances. The Tower's secrets were slipping through their fingers, and time was running out. Whatever the stakes, they were ready to face them—together.

Chapter 12: A Historical Puzzle

The morning light filtered through the narrow windows of the guest quarters as Max spread a collection of papers, old maps, and notes across the large table. His siblings gathered around, their faces tense with anticipation. Last night's discovery of the tampered security system had raised the stakes, and now the pressure was on to uncover the Tower's secrets before their mysterious adversary did.

"Okay, here's what we know so far," Max began, tapping his notebook. "The ghost's warning, the symbols Ava sketched, and the fragment of the Raven's Heart—all of it points to a hidden location somewhere in the Tower. I think I've found a way to figure out where."

He held up an old map he had found in the Tower's library, its edges yellowed and its markings faded. "This is a map of the Tower from the 15th century. Back then, some parts of the structure were still in use that are now sealed off."

"Like the hidden chamber you read about in that book," Emma said.

"Exactly," Max replied. "But the map alone isn't enough. That's where these come in." He gestured to several pages of historical documents, many written in dense, archaic handwriting. "These records mention renovations, secret passages, and storage areas that aren't on the modern maps. If we cross-reference the two, we might be able to figure out where the chamber is."

"Sounds like a lot of work," Leo said, leaning back in his chair.

"It's worth it," Sophie said. "If Max is right, this could lead us straight to the Raven's Heart."

The siblings worked together, poring over the documents and maps. Max guided the process, pointing out key details while Ava helped decipher some of the faded markings.

THE HAUNTED TOWER OF LONDON

"Look at this," Max said, pointing to a note scrawled in the margin of one map. "'Vault sealed under the White Tower, accessible only through the guardian's passage.'"

"Guardian's passage?" Sophie asked. "What's that?"

"It's mentioned here too," Ava said, holding up another document. "It says the passage was sealed centuries ago to protect the Tower's treasures."

"But if it was sealed, how are we supposed to get in?" Leo asked.

"There's a clue," Max said, holding up a third document. This one showed a diagram of the White Tower with a small, almost imperceptible mark near its base—a tiny emblem of a raven surrounded by a crown. "This matches the symbol Ava sketched and the one we found on the wall. It's got to be the entrance."

Emma leaned in, studying the map closely. "If we find that symbol near the White Tower, it could lead us to the passage. And if the passage is still intact, it might take us to the chamber."

"Then we have a plan," Sophie said, her eyes gleaming with excitement.

Later that day, the siblings made their way to the White Tower. Tourists still milled about, but the siblings stayed focused, scanning the stone walls for any sign of the emblem.

"There!" Ava said suddenly, pointing to a section of the wall near the base of the tower.

The others rushed to her side. Sure enough, the raven-and-crown symbol was etched into the stone, nearly invisible under centuries of grime.

"It's exactly like the one we found before," Max said, his excitement building. "This has to be the entrance."

Leo ran his fingers over the carving, searching for a mechanism. "There's got to be a way to open it."

"Wait," Emma said, pulling out the map. She compared the placement of the symbol to the diagram Max had pieced together.

"According to this, there's a specific sequence we need to activate. Look for other markings nearby."

Sophie found the next symbol, a smaller raven etched into the stone just a few feet away. She pressed it, and a faint grinding noise echoed through the air.

"It's working," she whispered.

Max found the third symbol, this one hidden under an overhanging stone. When he pressed it, the wall shifted slightly, revealing a narrow crack.

The siblings exchanged a glance.

"Here we go," Emma said, taking a deep breath.

The crack widened into an opening just large enough to squeeze through. Inside, the passage was dark and damp, the air heavy with the scent of stone and earth. The siblings turned on their flashlights, the beams cutting through the darkness.

"This must be the guardian's passage," Max said, his voice echoing slightly.

The corridor sloped downward, the walls narrowing as they moved deeper into the Tower's foundations. Strange symbols were carved into the stone, some matching the ones they had seen before.

"What do you think these mean?" Ava asked, running her fingers over one of the carvings.

"Probably warnings," Max said. "This whole place was designed to keep intruders out—or scare them away."

"Too late for that," Sophie said with a grin.

After several minutes of walking, the passage opened into a large, circular chamber. The walls were lined with stone shelves, and in the center of the room stood a pedestal, its surface covered in intricate carvings.

"Is this it?" Leo asked, his voice hushed.

Max stepped forward, his flashlight illuminating the pedestal. "It has to be. This is where the Raven's Heart would have been kept."

"But it's not here," Emma said, her tone grim. "If it was, it's been taken."

"Or hidden somewhere else," Max said. He noticed more symbols etched into the pedestal and began copying them into his notebook.

"What do you think they mean?" Sophie asked.

Max shook his head. "I'm not sure yet. But if we can figure it out, it might tell us where to go next."

As the siblings explored the chamber, a faint noise echoed through the passage—footsteps.

"Someone's coming," Leo whispered, his voice urgent.

Emma motioned for everyone to turn off their flashlights. They crouched in the shadows, their hearts pounding as the sound of footsteps grew louder.

Whoever was coming, they weren't alone in the Tower's secrets anymore.

Chapter 13: An Unexpected Ally

The siblings were still catching their breath from the close call in the hidden chamber when they were approached the next morning by a tall, bespectacled woman near the Tower's central courtyard. She wore a tailored grey coat and carried a leather satchel, her sharp eyes flicking over each of them with a mix of curiosity and caution.

"You're the Edmondson siblings, aren't you?" she asked, her voice smooth but deliberate.

Emma stepped forward, her guard up. "Who's asking?"

The woman gave a faint smile. "Dr. Evelyn Hargrove, Tower historian. Your parents mentioned you might be visiting. They told me you had a knack for... uncovering mysteries."

The mention of their parents made Emma relax slightly, though not entirely. "We've been doing some exploring," she admitted. "What's it to you?"

Dr. Hargrove glanced around, ensuring no one else was within earshot, before lowering her voice. "The Tower has always been a place of secrets, but recent events—strange disturbances, missing artifacts—have even the staff uneasy. I think you might have stumbled onto something important. Something I've been trying to figure out myself."

The siblings exchanged glances, their interest piqued but their wariness intact.

"What do you know about the Raven's Heart?" Max asked cautiously.

Dr. Hargrove's expression didn't change, but a flicker of recognition passed through her eyes. "More than most. The jewel has been the subject of speculation and legend for centuries, but few believe it ever truly existed. I take it you've found evidence to the contrary?"

Emma hesitated, debating how much to share. "We've found... clues," she said carefully. "Enough to think the jewel might still be here."

Dr. Hargrove nodded, her demeanour serious. "Then you're already ahead of most. But the Raven's Heart isn't just a treasure—it's a symbol of power and betrayal. If it's been disturbed, I can guarantee someone is after it. And they're not likely to stop until they have it."

"Why do you care?" Leo asked, his tone sceptical.

Dr. Hargrove's eyes narrowed slightly, but she kept her composure. "Because I've seen what happens when people dig too deeply into the Tower's secrets without understanding the risks. You're brave, but you're also young. If you want to survive this, you'll need help."

Despite her guarded demeanour, Dr. Hargrove seemed genuinely concerned. She offered to share her knowledge of the Tower's history, along with access to certain restricted records that even Max hadn't been able to find.

"This is everything I have on the Tower's hidden passages and sealed chambers," she said later that day, spreading a collection of aged documents and maps across a table in her office. "It's incomplete, but it might help you connect the dots."

Max dove into the materials immediately, his excitement bubbling over. "This map shows a secondary passage near the Queen's House! It's not on any of the modern blueprints."

"And this document," Ava said, pointing to a page, "mentions a key tied to the Raven's Heart. It says the key was hidden with the jewel's 'guardian.'"

"The ghost," Sophie murmured.

"It's all tied together," Emma said. "The ghost, the jewel, the missing artifacts—someone's been planning this for a long time."

As the siblings continued to piece together the puzzle, Dr. Hargrove watched them with an intensity that didn't go unnoticed.

"Why does it feel like you're not telling us everything?" Leo asked suddenly, his eyes narrowing at the historian.

Dr. Hargrove hesitated, her composure faltering for the first time. "Because some truths are dangerous," she said finally. "And because I'm not entirely sure who I can trust."

Emma straightened, her instincts flaring. "You know who's behind this, don't you?"

Dr. Hargrove didn't answer immediately. Instead, she stood and walked to the window, her gaze distant. "I have my suspicions. But I need proof before I say anything. If I'm wrong, the consequences could be disastrous—for all of us."

Despite her evasiveness, the siblings decided to work with Dr. Hargrove, if only because her knowledge of the Tower's history was invaluable. But Emma couldn't shake the feeling that the historian was keeping something vital from them.

As they left her office that evening, Sophie nudged Emma. "What do you think her deal is?"

"I don't know," Emma admitted. "But if she's hiding something, we'll figure it out. For now, let's use what she's given us. The map of the Queen's House passage might be our next lead."

Leo grinned. "Another hidden passage? Sounds like our kind of adventure."

Max looked thoughtful, his fingers tracing the edge of the map. "If the Raven's Heart is tied to the ghost, and the ghost is tied to betrayal... then whatever we find next might not just solve the mystery. It might explain why all of this is happening now."

"Then let's get to work," Emma said, her determination unshaken. "We're getting closer—I can feel it."

As they prepared for their next move, the siblings couldn't help but wonder: Was Dr. Hargrove an ally, or was she just another piece in the Tower's tangled web of secrets? Only time would tell.

Chapter 14: The Curse Revealed

Max hunched over the table in their quarters, his glasses sliding down his nose as he studied the ancient documents spread before him. The Tower historian, Dr. Hargrove, had given them access to a collection of old manuscripts, and Max had spent hours poring over the faded text. The siblings sat around him, anxiously waiting for any breakthrough.

"Okay," Max said, pushing his glasses up and looking at a particularly fragile parchment. "This is what I've found so far: the curse tied to the Raven's Heart doesn't just protect the jewel—it actively punishes anyone who tries to steal it or tamper with its power."

Sophie leaned forward, her elbows on the table. "Punishes how? Like spooky ghost punishments?"

"Worse," Max replied, his voice sombre. "According to these records, the Raven's Heart was created with a dual purpose: to protect the Tower and to expose betrayal. The alchemist, Elias Ravenscroft, infused it with a curse designed to ensure that any act of treachery would be revealed—no matter how long it took."

Ava tilted her head. "How does a jewel expose betrayal?"

Max tapped the parchment. "The curse manifests through what Ravenscroft called 'the Warden of Shadows.' It's a supernatural entity—probably the ghost we've seen—that appears when the jewel is stolen or its resting place is disturbed. The Warden's job is to lead the rightful guardians of the Tower to the truth, while punishing the traitors who betrayed it."

"That explains why the ghost pointed us toward the hidden chamber," Emma said, her tone thoughtful. "It's trying to help us find the Raven's Heart—and maybe the thief."

"But the thief already stole the Crown Jewels, didn't they?" Leo asked. "So why is the ghost still hanging around?"

Max turned the parchment toward the others, pointing to a section written in shaky, faded script. "This says that the Raven's Heart is the source of the curse's power. If the jewel is intact, the curse can function. But if the jewel is damaged or broken..."

"The curse breaks too," Emma finished, her expression grim. "That must be why the thief is trying so hard to find it. If they can destroy the Raven's Heart, the curse—and the ghost—will disappear."

A tense silence settled over the room as the siblings processed the implications.

"If the Raven's Heart is broken," Max continued, "it could also explain why the ghost seems weaker—appearing and disappearing, struggling to communicate."

"So the thief hasn't destroyed the whole jewel yet," Sophie said. "That means we still have a chance to stop them."

"But it also means they're close to finishing what they started," Leo added. "We need to move fast."

Max leaned back, running a hand through his hair. "There's one more thing," he said quietly.

"What?" Emma asked, her voice sharp.

Max hesitated, then pointed to another passage. "The curse doesn't just reveal betrayal—it enacts retribution. If the thief succeeds in destroying the jewel, the Tower itself might suffer. Ravenscroft designed the curse to protect the Tower, and without the Raven's Heart, it's vulnerable."

"You're saying the Tower could collapse?" Ava asked, her eyes wide.

"Not literally," Max said. "But its defences—both physical and mystical—would weaken. And since the Tower represents the strength of the kingdom, that could have... bigger consequences."

Emma stood, her jaw set with determination. "Then we can't let that happen. If the thief breaks the jewel, they're not just stealing a treasure—they're putting the entire Tower at risk."

Sophie grinned, her adrenaline already kicking in. "So what's the plan, boss?"

Emma glanced at Max, who nodded. "We need to use what we've learned about the curse—and the ghost—to track down the rest of the Raven's Heart. If we can find it before the thief does, we might be able to stop them."

"And if we don't?" Leo asked.

"Then the Tower—and everything it stands for—might not survive," Max said.

Ava looked at the group, her expression serious. "The ghost trusted us to figure this out. We can't let it down."

The siblings began to gather their supplies, their determination renewed. Max tucked the ancient parchment into his bag, its fragile script now etched into his memory. The curse had revealed its purpose: to protect the Tower, to expose betrayal, and to demand justice.

The ghost's appearances were no longer a mystery—they were a warning. And the Edmondsons knew it was up to them to answer the call.

With the Tower's history, their own courage, and the remnants of the Raven's Heart as their guide, they set out to uncover the final pieces of the puzzle before time ran out.

Chapter 15: Chasing Shadows

The Tower of London was cloaked in darkness as the siblings navigated its shadowy grounds, the air thick with tension. The faint glow of the moon barely illuminated the ancient walls, and the only sounds were the distant caws of the ravens and the crunch of gravel beneath their feet.

"We're getting close," Max whispered, clutching the parchment tightly. He had spent hours decoding the latest clue from the ghost's symbols, which hinted at a hidden location near the Bloody Tower.

"Stay sharp," Emma murmured, her flashlight beam scanning ahead. "If the ghost is leading us, we need to be ready for anything."

"I still think it's weird that we're trusting a ghost," Leo muttered, keeping pace. "What if it's setting us up?"

"It hasn't hurt us yet," Ava replied, her tone confident. "It's trying to help."

"Or it's playing us," Sophie added. "Guess we'll find out soon enough."

The siblings approached the Bloody Tower, its imposing silhouette looming over them. As they drew closer, a faint mist began to swirl around the entrance. The temperature dropped, and the air felt heavier.

"There it is," Sophie whispered, pointing.

A translucent figure hovered near the arched doorway, its form flickering like a dying flame. The ghost turned toward them, raising a hand as if beckoning them forward.

"It wants us to follow," Max said, his voice trembling with a mix of fear and excitement.

"Or it's leading us into a trap," Leo said again, his scepticism deepening.

Emma hesitated, her instincts warring with her curiosity. "We don't have a choice. If it knows where the Raven's Heart is, we need to follow it."

The siblings exchanged uneasy glances but nodded in agreement. Together, they stepped into the doorway, their flashlights barely penetrating the thickening mist.

The ghost led them through a narrow corridor that twisted deeper into the Tower's foundations. The walls were damp and cold, the air filled with the faint scent of mildew. The figure moved silently ahead of them, its glow casting eerie shadows on the stone.

"This place gives me the creeps," Ava said, clutching Emma's arm.

"Just keep moving," Emma said, her voice steady.

They followed the ghost into a large, circular chamber. At first glance, it seemed empty, but as their flashlights swept the room, they noticed strange markings on the walls—symbols similar to the ones Ava had sketched before.

"This has to be it," Max said, stepping forward to examine the carvings.

The ghost stopped in the center of the chamber, its form flickering violently before it vanished.

"Where did it go?" Sophie asked, spinning around.

"I don't know," Emma said, her unease growing.

Suddenly, a loud metallic clang echoed through the chamber. The siblings turned toward the entrance just in time to see a heavy iron gate slam shut, trapping them inside.

"It's a trap!" Leo shouted, rushing to the gate. He pushed against it, but it didn't budge.

From the shadows, a figure stepped forward—a tall, cloaked man with a smug expression.

"Well, well," the man said, his voice smooth and mocking. "The famous Edmondson siblings. I was wondering when you'd show up."

"Who are you?" Emma demanded, her eyes narrowing.

"Let's just say I'm someone with a vested interest in the Raven's Heart," the man replied. "And you've been meddling in my plans for far too long."

"Plans?" Max asked, his voice shaking. "You mean stealing the Raven's Heart?"

The man chuckled. "Stealing is such a crude term. Let's call it... reclaiming what should have been mine."

While the man spoke, Sophie's mind raced. Her eyes darted around the chamber, searching for anything that could help them escape. She noticed a loose stone in the wall near the gate, just big enough to wedge a tool into.

"Keep him talking," she whispered to Leo, slipping quietly toward the wall.

Leo nodded, stepping forward. "What makes you think you can control the Raven's Heart? It's cursed, you know."

The man's smile faltered for a moment. "Curses are just stories to keep fools away. The Raven's Heart is a source of power, and power is meant to be used."

As the man rambled, Sophie reached the loose stone and pulled a small multitool from her pocket. She wedged it into the crack and began to pry, her hands steady despite the adrenaline surging through her veins.

The stone shifted, revealing a narrow opening in the wall. Sophie peered through and saw a lever on the other side. She grinned.

"Emma," she hissed.

Emma glanced over and saw what Sophie was doing. She nodded subtly, then turned back to the man. "You're making a mistake," she said, her voice loud enough to cover Sophie's movements. "The Raven's Heart doesn't belong to you. It belongs to the Tower."

"And who's going to stop me?" the man sneered.

Sophie reached through the opening, her fingers brushing the lever. With a quick pull, the gate creaked and began to rise.

"Now!" Sophie shouted.

The siblings didn't hesitate. As the gate lifted, they bolted past the man, narrowly dodging his grasp.

"Stop them!" the man roared, but the siblings were already sprinting down the corridor.

They didn't stop until they were back in the open air, their lungs burning as they collapsed against a wall.

"That... was close," Leo panted.

"Too close," Emma said, her jaw tight. "That man—he's after the Raven's Heart, and he's not going to stop until he gets it."

"But now we know what we're up against," Max said. "And we know he's afraid of the curse. We can use that."

Sophie grinned, despite their close call. "At least we got out in one piece. Thanks to me."

Emma gave her a tired smile. "Good work, Sophie. But next time, let's try to avoid walking straight into a trap."

The siblings laughed nervously, their bond stronger than ever as they prepared for the next step in their quest. They had escaped the trap, but the game was far from over. The Raven's Heart—and the Tower's fate—still hung in the balance.

Chapter 16: A Stolen Artifact

Leo sat cross-legged on the floor of their quarters, his laptop balanced on his knees, the glow of the screen illuminating his face. His fingers flew over the keyboard as he sifted through surveillance footage, system logs, and network files he had managed to access during their nighttime escapades. The rest of the siblings were gathered around, waiting for any new lead.

"This guy has been messing with the security system for months," Leo muttered. "Whoever he is, he knows what he's doing. But I think I've found something."

"Let's hear it," Emma said, leaning forward.

Leo clicked on a video file, pulling up grainy footage from a camera positioned near the Jewel House. "This is from three nights ago," he explained. "Right around the time the ghost first started showing up regularly."

The footage showed a figure dressed in black slipping into the side entrance of the Jewel House. A few minutes later, they reemerged carrying a small, cloth-wrapped object. The figure moved swiftly, avoiding the main paths and slipping out of sight.

"What are they holding?" Ava asked, her eyes wide.

"I don't know," Leo said, rewinding the footage and zooming in on the object. It was blurry, but the shape was unmistakable—it looked like a small, jewelled sceptre.

"Could that be one of the stolen Crown Jewels?" Max asked.

"It has to be," Leo replied. "And there's more. Look at this."

He switched to another file, a log of outgoing data from the Tower's network. "Someone uploaded encrypted files to an external server right after this happened. I cracked part of it, and it looks like they were sending inventory records—detailed descriptions of specific jewels."

Emma's eyes narrowed. "They're cataloguing the missing artifacts. Why?"

"Probably to sell them," Sophie said, her tone disgusted. "You smuggle out a priceless artifact, then you auction it off to the highest bidder. It's the perfect crime—if you don't get caught."

Leo clicked through more footage, pulling up a third video. "This is from the security checkpoint near the Tower's outer gates. Look."

The siblings crowded closer as the footage showed the same cloaked figure passing through a back exit with a small duffel bag. The bag looked heavy, and the figure moved cautiously, avoiding the guards.

"They're smuggling it out," Emma said, her voice cold.

"Exactly," Leo said. "And judging by the timestamps, they managed to get the artifact out of the Tower the same night they stole it."

"But how did they sneak it past the guards?" Max asked. "The security here is supposed to be airtight."

Leo shook his head. "Not if you're controlling the system. The same person tampering with the cameras must have looped the footage and deactivated the sensors temporarily. It's all connected."

As they pieced together the evidence, Ava tapped her sketchbook thoughtfully. "If they've already smuggled out one artifact, does that mean they've taken more?"

"Not necessarily," Leo said. "The logs only show one item being moved off-site. But if they're targeting the Raven's Heart next, this was probably a test run. They wanted to see if they could get away with it."

Emma stood, pacing the room. "We need to figure out where that artifact went. If we can track it down, we might find out who's behind this—and how to stop them before they get to the Raven's Heart."

"Good luck tracking it," Sophie said. "Whoever this is, they've covered their tracks pretty well."

"Not completely," Leo said with a smirk, holding up a flash drive. "I copied part of the encryption keys they were using. It'll take some time, but I can trace the server they uploaded the files to. If we find the server, we might find the buyer—or at least their contact."

"You're a genius," Sophie said, grinning.

Leo shrugged. "I try."

While Leo worked on tracing the stolen artifact, Max examined the footage again, his brow furrowed. "It's strange," he said. "The way they handled that artifact—it looked almost... careful."

"Careful how?" Ava asked.

"Like they weren't just stealing it for money," Max said. "It's like they were protecting it, or maybe trying to preserve it for some other reason."

"You think this is about more than just theft?" Emma asked.

Max nodded. "If the Raven's Heart is as powerful as the legends say, it's possible the thief is collecting artifacts that could help them unlock its power—or neutralize its curse."

Later that evening, Leo leaned back from his laptop, a triumphant gleam in his eyes. "I've got something," he announced.

The siblings crowded around as Leo pulled up a map on the screen. "The files were sent to a server in Prague," he explained. "And guess what? The server belongs to a private auction house specializing in rare and illegal artifacts."

"So they're trying to sell it," Sophie said, her tone dark.

"Or they're using the auction as a cover to transport it to someone else," Max added.

Emma's expression was grim. "Either way, we need to stop them. If they're working this quickly, it won't be long before they move on the Raven's Heart."

The discovery of the stolen artifact was a critical breakthrough, but it also raised the stakes. The siblings now knew their enemy was not just after the Crown Jewels—they were orchestrating a larger plan, one that threatened the Tower and its history itself.

As they prepared for their next move, Emma spoke firmly, her voice steady. "We're not just solving a mystery anymore. We're protecting something bigger than us. And we're going to stop them—no matter what it takes."

The team nodded in agreement, their determination unwavering. The race to save the Raven's Heart—and the Tower—was on.

Chapter 17: Emma's Suspicions

The siblings regrouped in their quarters after another long day of investigations. The discovery of the stolen artifact had shaken them, but it had also lit a fire under their resolve. The Tower's secrets were unravelling, and Emma couldn't shake the nagging feeling that the answers were closer than they realized.

She paced the room, her arms crossed, her mind racing. "Something doesn't add up," she said finally, breaking the silence.

"What do you mean?" Max asked, looking up from his notebook.

"The thief," Emma replied. "They've been able to bypass security, smuggle an artifact out of one of the most heavily guarded places in the world, and stay ahead of us every step of the way. It doesn't make sense—unless they have help."

"Help from who?" Sophie asked.

"Someone inside," Emma said, her tone grim. "A member of the Tower staff."

The room fell silent as the siblings processed her words.

"You think it's an inside job?" Leo asked, his brow furrowed.

"It has to be," Emma said. "Think about it. They knew exactly when to disable the cameras and how to avoid the guards. They even knew about the hidden chamber. That's not something you can figure out from the outside."

Max flipped through his notes, nodding slowly. "It does explain how they've been able to move around so easily. The Tower is a maze, even for someone who studies it. They must have insider knowledge."

"And access," Leo added. "Someone who can move freely without raising suspicion."

"But who?" Ava asked. "There are so many staff members—guards, historians, maintenance workers. It could be anyone."

Emma sat down, her expression thoughtful. "We need to narrow it down. Think about the people we've encountered so far. Who's had the opportunity and the knowledge to pull this off?"

The siblings began listing the people they had interacted with since arriving at the Tower.

The guards: Professional but distracted, some had mentioned strange occurrences but seemed uninvolved.

The Ravenkeeper, Alistair: Knowledgeable about the Tower's history and the ravens' strange behaviour, but fiercely loyal to the Tower.

Dr. Evelyn Hargrove: The historian who had shared crucial information about the Tower's hidden passages and the Raven's Heart—but who also seemed to be hiding something.

"What about Dr. Hargrove?" Max suggested hesitantly. "She knows more about the Tower than anyone else we've met. And she was the one who gave us the documents about the Raven's Heart."

"She could be trying to steer us in the wrong direction," Sophie added.

Emma frowned. "Maybe. But she's also helped us. If she's involved, she's playing a very complicated game."

"Or she's covering her tracks," Leo said. "If she's the thief, it would make sense to stay close to us so she can control what we find out."

Emma rubbed her temples, feeling the weight of the decision. "We don't have enough proof to accuse anyone yet. But we can start paying closer attention—especially to Dr. Hargrove. Let's keep a record of everything she says and does from now on."

"What about the guards?" Sophie asked. "They're the ones who actually patrol the Jewel House."

"They're worth watching too," Emma said. "But most of them don't have the expertise to pull something like this off. Whoever the thief is, they're smart—probably someone with a background in history, archaeology, or security."

Ava tapped her sketchbook thoughtfully. "What if we try to figure out who has the most access? Like, who's been in the restricted areas recently?"

"That's a good idea," Max said. "We can cross-reference that with the locations where the ghost has appeared. If the thief is following the ghost's trail, they'll be going to the same places we've been."

The siblings spent the next few hours compiling a list of potential suspects and matching it against the Tower's layout.

By the end of the night, they had narrowed their focus to two individuals:

Dr. Evelyn Hargrove, the historian who seemed to know more about the Tower's secrets than she let on.

A senior security officer, whose patrol routes had coincided with key anomalies in the surveillance system.

"We need to keep an eye on both of them," Emma said, folding her arms. "If one of them is the thief, they'll make a move soon. And when they do, we'll be ready."

As the siblings settled in for the night, Emma stared out the window at the darkened Tower grounds. The pieces of the puzzle were falling into place, but the picture they formed was still murky.

She couldn't shake the feeling that they were being watched—by the thief, the ghost, or both. But whoever was behind the thefts and the tampering with the Raven's Heart, Emma was determined to stop them.

The Tower's secrets weren't just history—they were a responsibility. And Emma wasn't going to let the thief win.

Chapter 18: A Hidden Passage

The White Tower loomed above the siblings as they stood at its base, the ancient stones cold and silent in the late afternoon light. Ava was sketching a detailed rendering of the Tower's lower levels, her photographic memory helping her recreate the symbols and markings they had found earlier.

"If the hidden chamber is connected to the Raven's Heart, there's got to be another way in," Max said, poring over the map they had pieced together from historical records.

"I still think it's weird that we're relying on a map from centuries ago," Leo said, adjusting his backpack filled with tools. "What if this passage doesn't exist anymore?"

"Then we're out of luck," Emma replied, her voice steady. "But we have to try. Keep looking for anything unusual."

Ava's pencil paused mid-stroke. "Wait," she said softly, her eyes narrowing at the base of the Tower.

"What is it?" Sophie asked, stepping closer.

Ava pointed to a faint outline in the stone wall—barely visible unless you were looking directly at it. The lines formed a rectangular shape, suggesting the outline of a door. "That's not part of the original wall," Ava said.

Max leaned in, studying the markings. "She's right. The texture is different here—it's smoother, like it was added later."

"Could this be the entrance to another passage?" Emma asked.

"Only one way to find out," Leo said, pulling a small crowbar from his bag.

The siblings worked together, carefully prying at the edges of the stone outline. After a few tense minutes, there was a faint grinding noise as a hidden panel slid inward, revealing a dark, narrow staircase descending into the earth.

"Bingo," Sophie said, grinning.

Ava looked both excited and nervous. "Do you think the ghost will show up again?"

"Let's hope not," Emma said, switching on her flashlight. "Come on. We've come this far."

The staircase spiralled downward, the air growing colder and damper with each step. The siblings moved cautiously, their flashlights casting long shadows on the rough stone walls.

"This feels older than the rest of the Tower," Max said, his voice echoing in the confined space. "It might have been part of the original foundation."

At the bottom of the stairs, they found themselves in a narrow corridor lined with strange carvings—symbols similar to the ones Ava had sketched before.

"These markings are everywhere," Ava said, running her fingers over one. "Do you think they're warnings?"

"Or directions," Max said. "We should follow them."

The corridor led to a small, circular room. In the center stood a pedestal, much like the one they had found in the previous chamber. But this one was covered in dust and debris, as if it had been forgotten for centuries.

"This must be the room," Emma said, stepping forward.

The pedestal was engraved with intricate designs, including the same raven-and-crown emblem they had seen throughout their search. But unlike the other pedestal, this one had a shallow depression in its surface, shaped like a jewel.

"The Raven's Heart," Max whispered. "This is where it was kept."

"But it's not here now," Sophie said, her voice tinged with frustration.

"No, but this might still give us a clue," Max said, shining his flashlight over the carvings.

Ava knelt beside the pedestal, her sharp eyes catching something the others had missed—a small latch hidden beneath the edge of the stone. "There's a compartment here," she said, reaching for it.

The siblings held their breath as Ava carefully pulled the latch. A section of the pedestal slid open, revealing a hidden drawer. Inside was a rolled-up piece of parchment and a small, tarnished metal key.

"Good find, Ava," Emma said, her voice filled with pride.

Max unrolled the parchment, his hands trembling slightly. It was covered in more of the strange symbols, along with a crude map showing what appeared to be another chamber deeper within the Tower's foundations.

"This map—it's pointing to somewhere below the Bloody Tower," Max said, his excitement building.

"And the key might be for the entrance," Ava added, holding it up.

As they examined their findings, the faint sound of footsteps echoed from the corridor behind them.

"Someone's coming," Leo whispered.

Emma motioned for them to stay quiet, extinguishing their flashlights. The footsteps grew louder, and a shadow appeared at the top of the stairs.

"Quick, hide," Emma hissed.

The siblings ducked behind the pedestal, their hearts pounding as the shadowy figure entered the room.

The figure paused, their head turning as if sensing they weren't alone. For a tense moment, the room was silent except for the faint drip of water from the ceiling.

Then the figure turned and left, their footsteps retreating up the stairs.

"That was too close," Sophie said, exhaling shakily.

"They're looking for the same thing we are," Emma said, her voice low. "And they're getting closer. We need to move fast."

With the map and key in hand, the siblings made their way back to the surface, their determination stronger than ever. The hidden passage had revealed another piece of the puzzle, but it also confirmed their worst fears—the thief was one step ahead of them.

"We have to find the next chamber before they do," Emma said as they emerged into the cold night air.

"And this time," Ava said, clutching the key tightly, "we're not letting them beat us."

The Tower's secrets were coming to light, and the race to uncover the truth was more urgent than ever. The Raven's Heart—and the Tower's future—depended on it.

Chapter 19: The Ghost Speaks

The Tower of London seemed even more oppressive in the stillness of night. The siblings huddled near the base of the Bloody Tower, their nerves on edge. The hidden passage beneath the White Tower had led them to a new map and a mysterious key, but the next step in their journey remained unclear.

"It has to be here," Max said, studying the map under the faint glow of his flashlight. "This spot—below the Bloody Tower—is marked as a significant location, but there's no clear entrance."

"Maybe we missed something," Ava suggested, her eyes scanning the ground for any hidden markings.

Emma frowned, her instincts tingling. "If the ghost really is tied to the Raven's Heart, it might show up again to guide us."

"I'd rather not rely on a ghost," Leo muttered. "But we don't have much choice."

As if on cue, a faint chill swept through the air, and a soft glow appeared near the Tower's entrance. The siblings froze as the translucent figure materialized, its form flickering and shifting like smoke caught in the wind.

"It's back," Sophie whispered, her voice a mix of awe and fear.

The ghost hovered silently for a moment, its misty hand raised as though beckoning them forward. Then it drifted toward the base of the Tower, stopping near a low, crumbling section of the wall.

"It's pointing at something," Max said, stepping cautiously closer.

The siblings followed the ghost's gesture, their flashlights illuminating the rough stonework. Ava's sharp eyes caught it first—a faint outline of a small compartment hidden within the wall.

"There's something here," she said, running her fingers over the edges of the stone.

With a bit of effort, Leo managed to pry open the compartment, revealing a dusty, leather-bound book inside. Max carefully pulled it out, his hands trembling slightly.

"It's a diary," he said, brushing away the cobwebs. The faded cover bore the initials T.G.

"Who's T.G.?" Sophie asked.

Max opened the book, flipping through the brittle pages. The handwriting was cramped and uneven, but the entries were legible. "It's written by a Tower guard from the late 1600s," he said. "Thomas Grey. He was assigned to protect the Crown Jewels."

"Let me guess," Emma said, her voice steady. "He wrote about the Raven's Heart."

Max nodded, excitement building as he read aloud. "'The jewel known as the Raven's Heart is no ordinary treasure. It carries a curse upon any who would steal it, and I have witnessed its effects firsthand. One of my fellow guards attempted to take it, and he was struck down within hours. His cries haunted the Tower for days.'"

"That explains the ghost," Ava said. "The Warden of Shadows."

Max continued flipping through the diary until he reached a section marked with an ink blot, as though the writer had hesitated before continuing. "'The chamber beneath the Bloody Tower holds more than just the jewel. It is a place of judgment, where those who betray their oaths are confronted by their sins. I have been sworn to protect its secrets, but I fear my loyalty will be tested.'"

The siblings exchanged uneasy glances.

"Sounds like he was afraid of something," Sophie said.

"Or someone," Emma added.

Max turned to the final entry in the diary. "'Tonight, I feel the weight of the Tower's history upon me. The Raven's Heart is stirring, and I cannot ignore its call. If this is my last account, let it be known: the key lies not in the stone, but in the truth. Only those who face it will prevail.'"

"The truth?" Ava repeated. "What does that mean?"

"It could be a metaphor," Max said. "Or it could be literal. The key might not just open a door—it might reveal something important."

"The diary itself might be the clue," Emma said. "Thomas Grey clearly knew about the Raven's Heart, and he left this behind for a reason. We need to study it more closely."

The ghost lingered a moment longer, its form dimming as though its energy was fading. Then it raised its hand one final time, pointing toward the Tower's interior.

"It's leading us again," Sophie said, standing.

"We'll follow," Emma said, clutching the diary tightly. "But we'll be ready this time."

As the siblings moved deeper into the Tower, guided by the ghost's flickering presence, they couldn't shake the feeling that the answers they sought were closer than ever—and that the Tower's secrets were finally coming to light.

The diary was more than just a record; it was a warning, a guide, and a key to the truth. But the question remained: would the truth be enough to stop the thief—and the curse?

Chapter 20: Betrayal Uncovered

The siblings huddled around the small table in their quarters, the dim glow of a single lamp casting shadows across their faces. The diary of Thomas Grey lay open, its fragile pages revealing unsettling truths about the Raven's Heart and the cursed chamber beneath the Tower. Yet, even as they pored over the text, Emma couldn't ignore the growing doubt gnawing at the back of her mind.

Dr. Evelyn Hargrove had been helpful—too helpful. She had provided them with critical maps, historical records, and insights, yet her guarded demeanour and occasional evasiveness had begun to raise red flags.

"She knows more than she's letting on," Emma said, her voice low but firm. "I've been trying to ignore it, but something doesn't add up."

"You think she's working with the thief?" Leo asked, raising an eyebrow.

"It's possible," Emma replied. "She has access to everything—the Tower's archives, restricted areas, and even the staff schedules. If anyone could pull this off, it's her."

"She's also the one who told us about the Raven's Heart in the first place," Max pointed out. "Why would she do that if she's trying to steal it?"

"To keep us distracted," Sophie suggested. "If she's leading us in circles, we're not getting in her way."

The room fell silent as the siblings considered the possibility. Ava broke the silence, her voice quiet but resolute. "How do we prove it?"

Emma tapped the table thoughtfully. "We start by checking her movements. She's been spending a lot of time in the restricted areas lately. If we can catch her in the act, we'll have our answer."

"Or we'll get caught ourselves," Leo muttered, earning a sharp look from Emma.

The next morning, the siblings kept a discreet distance as they shadowed Dr. Hargrove through the Tower grounds. She moved with purpose, carrying her ever-present satchel of documents and stopping occasionally to converse with guards or staff.

"She's definitely up to something," Sophie whispered as they watched her enter the Jewel House.

"Let's move," Emma said, leading the way toward the building.

Inside, they found Dr. Hargrove standing near one of the displays, her back to them. She was speaking in hushed tones to a tall man in a dark uniform—a senior security officer they had seen before.

"Didn't we tag him as a possible suspect?" Max asked, his voice barely audible.

Emma nodded. "Keep listening."

The siblings crept closer, staying hidden behind a column.

"...need to ensure everything is in place," Dr. Hargrove was saying. "We're running out of time."

The officer nodded. "The artifact will be moved tonight. Are you sure the distraction will hold?"

"It will," Dr. Hargrove replied, her tone cold. "The children are resourceful, but they're playing right into our hands."

Ava's gasp was barely stifled by Sophie's quick hand. Emma clenched her fists, anger and betrayal roiling inside her.

"They're working together," Leo whispered, his jaw tightening. "She's been playing us this whole time."

The siblings slipped out of the Jewel House and regrouped in a quiet corner of the Tower grounds. Emma's mind raced as she pieced together the implications.

"If they're moving the artifact tonight," she said, her voice steady despite her fury, "that means they're close to finishing whatever they're planning."

"And they're using us to cover their tracks," Max added. "They've been letting us chase the ghost and the diary while they focus on stealing the Raven's Heart."

"We have to stop them," Sophie said, her eyes blazing.

"We will," Emma said firmly. "But we need a plan. If we confront them now, they'll just deny it—and we'll lose our chance to catch them in the act."

After a quick strategy session, the siblings decided to split up. Max and Ava would return to their quarters to study the diary for any additional clues, while Emma, Sophie, and Leo would keep a close watch on Dr. Hargrove and the security officer.

As they moved into position, Emma felt a renewed sense of determination. They had trusted Dr. Hargrove, but she had betrayed that trust. Now, it was up to them to protect the Tower—and the Raven's Heart—from falling into the wrong hands.

That evening, as the shadows lengthened and the Tower grew quiet, the siblings prepared to confront their adversaries. The truth was out, and the stakes had never been higher.

Dr. Hargrove's betrayal had cut deep, but it had also given them the clarity they needed. The Tower's secrets would not remain hidden much longer, and the Edmondsons were ready to face whatever came next.

Chapter 21: Decoding the Diary

The quiet hum of the lamp filled the room as Max and Ava sat at the table, the fragile pages of Thomas Grey's diary spread between them. Outside, the Tower of London loomed in silence, its ancient stones holding secrets that seemed to whisper through the walls. The weight of their mission pressed heavily on the siblings, but Ava's sharp eyes and Max's analytical mind kept them focused.

"This diary has to be hiding something," Max said, his fingers gently tracing the worn edges of the pages. "Thomas Grey wouldn't have written so cryptically unless he wanted to keep the information safe."

Ava leaned over, studying the cramped handwriting. "The part about 'the key lies not in the stone, but in the truth'—what if he's talking about more than just a physical key?"

"You mean, like a code?" Max asked, his excitement building.

"Exactly," Ava said. "Look here—he uses certain words over and over: 'guardian,' 'truth,' 'oath.' It's like he's emphasizing something."

The siblings dove into the text, searching for patterns. Ava's photographic memory helped her recall specific phrases, while Max used a small notepad to jot down repeated words and phrases.

"Here," Ava said, pointing to a section near the middle of the diary. "'The chamber beneath the Bloody Tower is guarded not by stone, but by those who serve their oaths. Their names hold the truth.'"

Max's eyes lit up. "Names! What if the key to the location isn't an object, but a name or sequence of names? The guards who served the Tower might have left clues."

"Let's cross-reference this with the other sections," Ava suggested.

As they worked, Max began to notice a subtle pattern. Certain letters in the text were slightly darker, as if the writer had pressed the quill harder on those strokes.

"Look at this," Max said, circling a line in the diary. "'The light will reveal what the shadow cannot hide.' That has to mean something."

Ava tilted her head thoughtfully. "What if he's hiding something in plain sight? Like invisible ink or faint markings?"

Max nodded and grabbed a small flashlight from his bag. He shone the beam at an angle across the page, and faintly, a series of numbers and letters appeared beneath the text.

"You were right!" Max exclaimed. "It's a code."

The siblings quickly transcribed the hidden message, which read:

T.G. 7/4 B.T. NW corner

"T.G. has to be Thomas Grey," Ava said. "And 'B.T.' must mean the Bloody Tower."

"'NW corner'—the northwest corner of the Bloody Tower," Max added. "That must be where he hid something."

"But what about the 7/4?" Ava asked, frowning.

"It could be a date or a sequence," Max speculated. "Either way, it's another clue."

With their discovery in hand, the siblings rushed to find Emma, Sophie, and Leo. They were keeping watch near the Bloody Tower, tracking Dr. Hargrove and the suspicious security officer.

"We found it!" Ava said breathlessly as they arrived. "The diary—it had a hidden code pointing to the northwest corner of the Bloody Tower."

Emma's eyes narrowed. "That has to be where the stolen jewels are hidden—or where the Raven's Heart is."

"Either way, we need to get there before they do," Max said.

The group moved quickly but cautiously, using the shadows to stay out of sight. As they approached the Bloody Tower's northwest corner, the tension in the air was palpable.

"This is it," Max whispered, pointing to a section of the wall that matched the description in the diary.

Ava knelt down, her fingers feeling along the edges of the stone. "There's a loose brick here."

With Leo's help, she carefully pried the brick loose, revealing a small, hidden compartment. Inside was a dusty velvet pouch tied with a frayed ribbon.

Emma carefully opened it, and the siblings gasped. Inside were several gleaming jewels, their intricate designs unmistakable.

"The stolen artifacts," Sophie said, her voice hushed.

As they marvelled at their discovery, footsteps echoed nearby.

"They're coming," Leo hissed, his eyes scanning the shadows.

Emma quickly handed the pouch to Ava. "Hide it, now," she whispered.

Ava slipped the pouch into her jacket just as Dr. Hargrove and the security officer rounded the corner.

"What are you doing here?" Dr. Hargrove demanded, her voice sharp.

Emma stepped forward, her expression calm but defiant. "Just admiring the Tower's history. What about you?"

Dr. Hargrove's eyes flicked to the section of the wall they had disturbed, but her face remained composed. "Nothing that concerns you."

The tension between them crackled like static, but Emma held her ground. Dr. Hargrove and her accomplice exchanged a brief glance before retreating into the shadows.

As soon as they were gone, Emma turned to the group. "We have the stolen jewels, but we're not safe yet. They know we're onto them."

"What do we do now?" Ava asked, clutching her jacket tightly.

Emma's jaw tightened. "We keep moving. If the jewels were here, the Raven's Heart can't be far. And we're not letting them beat us to it."

With the diary's code cracked and the stolen jewels in their possession, the siblings knew they were closer than ever to uncovering the Tower's ultimate secret. But the stakes had never been higher, and the final confrontation was looming.

Chapter 22: Sabotage

The morning after recovering the stolen jewels, the siblings gathered in their quarters to plan their next move. Leo was hunched over his laptop, connecting it to an array of devices and tools he had brought along. The equipment had been essential in cracking the security system, tracking anomalies, and uncovering hidden passages within the Tower.

"This should only take a few minutes," Leo said, glancing up at his siblings. "Once I sync this with the footage from last night, we might be able to figure out where Dr. Hargrove and her accomplice went after they left the Bloody Tower."

"You're a wizard, Leo," Sophie said, leaning against the wall. "Keep it up."

Ava was sketching in her notebook while Max pored over Thomas Grey's diary for any additional clues. Emma stood near the window, scanning the Tower grounds below for any signs of suspicious activity.

Suddenly, Leo let out a frustrated groan. "What the—?"

"What's wrong?" Emma asked, turning sharply.

Leo pointed at his laptop screen, which had gone dark. "Something's not right. The system isn't booting up."

"Maybe it's just a glitch," Max suggested.

Leo shook his head, pulling his equipment closer for inspection. "No way. This isn't random. Look at this." He held up a small cable that had been sliced cleanly in half. "Someone tampered with my gear."

The room went silent as the implications sank in.

"Who would do that?" Ava asked, her voice barely above a whisper.

"Take a wild guess," Sophie said, crossing her arms. "Dr. Hargrove and her buddy probably snuck in last night while we were busy."

"But how would they get in here without us noticing?" Max asked. "We've been watching them."

"Not closely enough," Emma said, her voice tight with frustration. "They must've been keeping tabs on us, waiting for the right moment to strike."

Leo set the damaged cable aside and began sifting through the rest of his equipment. "It's not just the cable," he said grimly. "The hard drive I was using to store all our footage and logs? It's gone."

"What?" Sophie exclaimed, her voice rising.

"They took it," Leo said, his tone cold. "Everything we've recorded—all the anomalies, the security glitches, the proof of what they've been doing—it's all gone."

"Without that footage, we don't have any evidence," Max said, sinking into a chair. "It's their word against ours."

Emma's jaw clenched. "They're trying to slow us down. They know we're getting close, and they're desperate to throw us off."

Leo ran a hand through his hair, his frustration mounting. "I can fix most of this, but it's going to take time. I'll need to rebuild the system and replace some of the components. Until then, we're flying blind."

"We don't have time," Sophie said, pacing the room. "If they're already sabotaging us, they're probably making their move on the Raven's Heart right now."

Emma stepped forward, her voice steady. "Then we work without the equipment. Leo, do what you can to get us back online, but the rest of us will keep investigating. We'll rely on the maps, the diary, and our instincts. If they think this is going to stop us, they're wrong."

As Leo set to work repairing his equipment, the others reviewed their notes and maps, trying to piece together their next move. Ava studied the diary again, her sharp eyes catching a detail they had overlooked before.

"Look at this," she said, pointing to an entry in Thomas Grey's handwriting. "'When the shadows grow long, the final truth will be revealed.'"

"What does that mean?" Max asked, leaning over to read.

"It could be a reference to time," Ava said. "Like sunset."

Emma nodded. "That fits with the ghost's behaviour. It always appears at dusk. If we're going to find the Raven's Heart, that might be the time to do it."

As the day wore on, the tension in the room grew. Leo worked tirelessly to repair the damage, his frustration bubbling under the surface. Meanwhile, Emma led the others in finalizing their plan to intercept Dr. Hargrove and her accomplice before they could take the Raven's Heart.

"This isn't just about stopping them," Emma said. "It's about protecting the Tower and everything it represents. We can't let them win."

By the time sunset approached, Leo had managed to restore part of his system, though the hard drive with their most critical data was still missing. He joined the others near the Bloody Tower, his determination undimmed despite the setback.

"They might've slowed us down," Leo said, adjusting his backpack, "but they haven't stopped us."

"Good," Emma said, her eyes fixed on the darkening sky. "Because this ends tonight."

The siblings exchanged determined glances. The sabotage had been a blow, but it hadn't broken them. They were ready for whatever lay ahead—and they weren't going to let anything, or anyone, stand in their way.

Chapter 23: The Chase Begins

The air was cold and sharp as the Edmondson siblings stood outside a nondescript warehouse on the edge of London. The trail they had pieced together from the stolen jewels and Max's decoding of Thomas Grey's diary had led them here. The building looked abandoned, its cracked windows and rusted doors suggesting years of neglect.

"Are we sure this is the right place?" Sophie asked, her eyes scanning the darkened structure.

"It has to be," Max replied, clutching the map. "The trail ends here—or at least, it should."

"Let's not stand around waiting to get caught," Emma said firmly. "Stay close, and keep your eyes open."

The siblings slipped through a side door, their footsteps echoing in the cavernous space. The interior was as desolate as the exterior, with piles of broken crates and discarded tools scattered across the floor. Dust hung heavy in the air, illuminated by the faint beams of moonlight streaming through the broken windows.

"This place gives me the creeps," Ava whispered, staying close to Sophie.

Leo moved ahead, his flashlight cutting through the shadows. "If the thief was here, they didn't leave much behind."

"Spread out," Emma instructed. "Look for anything that seems out of place."

The siblings fanned out, combing the warehouse for clues. Max searched through a stack of old papers, while Ava examined a row of broken shelves. Leo and Sophie checked the perimeter, their eyes peeled for hidden compartments or signs of recent activity.

"I've got something," Sophie called, her voice echoing slightly.

The others hurried to her side. She was crouched near a large wooden crate, its lid partially pried open. Inside was a pile of discarded tools—and a single velvet pouch.

Emma carefully lifted the pouch, her breath catching as she opened it. Inside was a small, polished gemstone—one of the stolen jewels.

"They were here," Emma said, her tone sharp. "But why would they leave this behind?"

"It could be a trap," Leo suggested. "Or they had to leave in a hurry."

Max picked up a piece of paper from the crate, his brow furrowing as he read it. "It's a receipt. For delivery to the Tower."

"What?" Ava asked, peering over his shoulder.

Max held up the slip, his voice tense. "It's dated today. Whoever was here took something back to the Tower."

The siblings exchanged uneasy glances.

"This was a decoy," Emma said, realization dawning. "They led us here to throw us off their trail while they moved whatever they're after back to the Tower."

"They're going for the Raven's Heart," Max said, his voice urgent. "It's the only thing left."

Without wasting another second, the siblings raced back to the Tower. The city lights blurred past them as they hurried through the streets, their hearts pounding.

"We're running out of time," Emma said as they approached the Tower's gates. "If we don't stop them now, they'll finish what they started."

"They've been one step ahead of us this whole time," Sophie said. "How do we catch them now?"

Emma's jaw tightened. "We follow the clues. They're headed to the hidden chamber beneath the Bloody Tower. That has to be where the Raven's Heart is."

As they entered the Tower grounds, the siblings slowed their pace, their senses on high alert. The familiar shadows of the ancient walls seemed darker, heavier, as though the Tower itself was holding its breath.

"This way," Max whispered, leading them toward the entrance to the hidden passage they had discovered earlier.

The door was ajar, its heavy iron latch hanging loosely.

"They're already inside," Leo said grimly.

The siblings descended into the depths of the Tower, the air growing colder with each step. The faint sound of voices echoed from ahead, drawing them deeper into the passage.

As they rounded a corner, Emma held up a hand, signalling for the others to stop. Ahead of them, in the dim light of the hidden chamber, stood Dr. Evelyn Hargrove and the security officer. Between them rested the pedestal, and on it lay a fragment of the Raven's Heart, glowing faintly in the dark.

"They've got it," Ava whispered, her voice trembling.

"Not for long," Emma replied, her eyes blazing. "Let's end this."

The siblings exchanged determined glances before stepping into the chamber, ready to confront the thieves and protect the Tower's most guarded secret. The chase was over, but the fight was just beginning.

Chapter 24: A Ghostly Protector

The chamber beneath the Bloody Tower echoed with tension as the Edmondson siblings faced Dr. Evelyn Hargrove and the security officer, who stood flanking the Raven's Heart fragment. Its faint glow illuminated the thieves' faces, their expressions a mixture of triumph and desperation.

Emma's voice was sharp as a blade. "Step away from the Raven's Heart."

Dr. Hargrove's smile was cold. "You're brave, I'll give you that. But bravery alone won't stop us."

"You don't understand what you're dealing with," Max said, his voice steady despite the fear bubbling beneath the surface. "The curse isn't just a story—it's real."

"Enough stalling," the security officer growled, stepping forward. He pointed a small device toward the siblings—a disruptor, designed to jam their equipment. "You're not leaving here with that jewel."

Before anyone could respond, the faint glow of the Raven's Heart intensified, and the air in the chamber grew cold. A low, mournful wail echoed through the space, sending shivers down everyone's spine.

The ghost appeared.

The translucent figure emerged from the shadows, its misty form flickering with an otherworldly energy. Its hollow eyes focused on the thieves, its presence filling the chamber with a palpable sense of dread.

"What is this?" the security officer shouted, stumbling backward.

Dr. Hargrove's face paled. "The Warden of Shadows," she whispered, her voice trembling. "It can't be..."

The ghost raised a spectral hand, and the glow of the Raven's Heart pulsed in response. The thieves froze, rooted to the spot as if an invisible force was holding them in place.

"Now's our chance!" Emma shouted. "Go, Sophie—get the fragment!"

Sophie darted forward, her agile movements a blur as she reached the pedestal. But just as her fingers brushed the Raven's Heart, the security officer broke free from his paralysis and lunged toward her.

"Sophie, look out!" Ava screamed.

The officer grabbed Sophie's arm, yanking her back. She struggled, her heart racing as the pedestal loomed just out of reach. The man's grip tightened, and for a moment, it seemed she wouldn't escape.

Then the ghost intervened.

The air crackled with energy as the ghost surged forward, its misty form solidifying just enough to pry the officer's hand from Sophie's arm. The man stumbled backward, his eyes wide with terror as the ghost loomed over him.

"Run!" the ghost's voice boomed, echoing through the chamber like the tolling of a bell.

Sophie didn't need to be told twice. She grabbed the fragment of the Raven's Heart and sprinted back toward her siblings. The ghost turned its attention to the thieves, its spectral form blocking their path.

The siblings raced up the narrow passageway, Sophie clutching the fragment tightly. Behind them, the ghost's wails grew louder, mingling with the panicked shouts of Dr. Hargrove and the officer.

"Did you hear that?" Ava asked breathlessly as they climbed. "The ghost—it spoke!"

"It's more than just a ghost," Max said, his voice filled with awe. "It's protecting the Raven's Heart—and us."

"But why?" Sophie asked, her heart still pounding from the narrow escape.

Emma's voice was calm but resolute. "Because it knows we're not the threat. We're trying to save the Tower, just like it is."

As they emerged into the cold night air, the siblings paused to catch their breath. The fragment in Sophie's hands glowed faintly, its energy pulsing like a heartbeat.

"What do we do now?" Leo asked.

"We protect this fragment at all costs," Emma said. "The ghost saved us for a reason. It knows we're the only ones who can stop them."

"And maybe," Max added, glancing back toward the hidden passage, "it's trying to tell us something more."

The ghost's intervention had shifted everything. It wasn't just a supernatural guardian; it was an ally in their fight to protect the Tower. But as the siblings prepared for the final confrontation, one question lingered in their minds: Who—or what—was the Warden of Shadows, and what role did it play in the Tower's deepest secrets?

The answers were closer than ever, but so was the danger. The Raven's Heart wasn't just a treasure—it was the key to a mystery centuries in the making. And the siblings were about to uncover the truth.

Chapter 25: The Family Secret

The siblings gathered in their quarters, their adrenaline still high from the narrow escape in the hidden chamber. Sophie placed the fragment of the Raven's Heart carefully on the table, its faint glow casting flickering shadows across their faces.

"This changes everything," Max said, staring at the fragment. "The ghost isn't just some curse. It's trying to guide us—and it saved Sophie. It's protecting this."

Emma didn't respond immediately. She had been quiet since they returned, her thoughts distant. As the others debated the next steps, her mind replayed the ghost's actions, the eerie way it had seemed almost familiar.

"Emma?" Ava's voice pulled her from her thoughts. "Are you okay?"

Emma took a deep breath. "I think there's something we're missing. Something bigger. This isn't just about the Raven's Heart or the Tower—it's connected to us."

"What do you mean?" Sophie asked.

Emma reached into her bag and pulled out a worn notebook bound in dark leather. It had belonged to their mother, Dr. Eleanor Edmondson, a renowned archaeologist who had dedicated her career to uncovering the secrets of ancient artifacts.

"This was Mom's," Emma said, placing it on the table. "I didn't think much of it before, but when we were in the chamber, something about the ghost—about this fragment—felt... familiar."

She opened the notebook, flipping through pages of handwritten notes, sketches, and references to historical artifacts. Finally, she stopped at a page titled: The Raven's Heart: Legend or Reality?

"What?" Max leaned closer, his eyes wide. "Mom was researching the Raven's Heart?"

"She didn't just research it," Emma said, her voice steady. "She was trying to find it."

The siblings crowded around the notebook as Emma read aloud.

"The Raven's Heart, said to protect the Tower of London, is more than a legend. Its connection to the Tower's history is undeniable, but its true purpose remains hidden. I believe it is a key—not just to the Tower's secrets, but to something far older."

"Far older?" Leo repeated, frowning. "What does that mean?"

Emma flipped to another page, revealing a sketch of the Raven's Heart surrounded by symbols—the same symbols they had seen in the hidden chambers. "She thought the Raven's Heart wasn't just cursed. It was designed to protect something—something ancient and powerful."

Sophie leaned back, her brow furrowed. "But why didn't she ever tell us about this?"

"Because she thought it was dangerous," Emma said, pointing to a note scrawled in the margin: 'The Warden of Shadows is no mere guardian. It is bound to the jewel by a pact, one that cannot be broken without great cost.'

Ava's voice trembled. "The ghost—the Warden—is bound to the Raven's Heart?"

Max nodded, his mind racing. "That explains why it's trying to protect it. If the Raven's Heart is destroyed, the Warden's purpose ends."

As they processed the revelation, Emma turned to the last entry in the notebook. The handwriting was hurried, almost frantic.

"I've traced the artifact's history to the Tower, but the trail ends there. If the Raven's Heart is still intact, it must be hidden beneath the Bloody Tower. But there's another layer to this mystery—one I dare not pursue without more proof. If my children ever find this, know that I did this to protect them. The truth is dangerous, but it must be uncovered."

The room fell silent.

"She knew," Ava whispered. "She knew we'd find this one day."

Emma closed the notebook, her expression resolute. "This isn't just a mission anymore. It's personal. Mom believed the Raven's Heart held the key to something bigger, and now it's up to us to finish what she started."

Leo broke the silence. "But if Mom thought this was so dangerous, why would she want us involved?"

"Because she trusted us to do the right thing," Emma said. "She trusted us to protect the Tower—and whatever the Raven's Heart is hiding—from people like Dr. Hargrove."

Max's voice was quiet but determined. "Then we can't let her down."

The siblings spent the next few hours poring over the notebook, connecting their mother's research to everything they had discovered so far. Dr. Eleanor Edmondson's notes hinted at a hidden mechanism tied to the Raven's Heart, one that could reveal the jewel's true purpose—but only if the artifact was intact.

"We need to figure out how this fragment fits into the bigger picture," Emma said. "And we need to stop Dr. Hargrove before she destroys it."

"She thinks she's in control," Sophie said. "But she doesn't know we've got the notebook—and the fragment."

Emma nodded. "And we're going to use both to end this."

As the siblings prepared for their next move, the glow of the Raven's Heart fragment seemed to pulse with energy, as if responding to their resolve. The Tower's secrets, their mother's legacy, and the truth behind the Warden of Shadows were all within reach—but so was the danger.

The Edmondsons weren't just solving a mystery anymore. They were stepping into their family's history, and the stakes had never been higher.

Chapter 26: The Jewel's Power

The Raven's Heart fragment lay on the table in their quarters, its faint glow casting an otherworldly light across the room. Max sat with the family notebook open in front of him, flipping through its pages while the others gathered around. Each discovery about the jewel seemed to raise more questions, but this time, the stakes were higher than ever.

Max tapped a page with an intricate drawing of the Raven's Heart, surrounded by the same symbols they had seen etched into the Tower's walls. "Listen to this," he said, reading aloud. "'The Raven's Heart is not just a jewel. It is a conduit, capable of channelling energy tied to an ancient pact. Its glow is said to reveal hidden truths and grant power to those deemed worthy—but only at a cost.'"

"A cost?" Ava asked, her voice tinged with worry.

Max nodded. "According to Mom's notes, the jewel's power is linked to the Warden of Shadows and the Tower itself. The pact binds all three together: the jewel, the guardian, and the place it was meant to protect. If the Raven's Heart is removed or destroyed, the pact collapses."

"And the Tower falls," Emma said, her voice steady but grim.

"But it's not just about the Tower," Max continued, flipping to another section. "Mom traced the jewel's origins back to ancient myths—stories about artifacts that could manipulate light, energy, and even time."

"Time?" Sophie said, raising an eyebrow. "You're saying this thing is a time machine?"

Max shook his head. "Not exactly. It's more like... a beacon. It can reveal hidden paths, secret chambers, and lost knowledge. But only someone who understands the pact can wield it without triggering the curse."

Leo leaned forward, his brow furrowed. "And let me guess—Dr. Hargrove doesn't understand the pact. She's just after the power."

"Exactly," Max said. "If she tries to use the jewel without understanding the consequences, it could destroy her—and the Tower."

"So we're dealing with a cursed treasure that can reveal secret truths and potentially bring down an ancient building," Sophie said, smirking. "No pressure."

Emma ignored her sister's humour, her mind racing. "If the Raven's Heart is this powerful, that explains why the Warden is so desperate to protect it—and why the ghost saved Sophie."

"It also means we can't let Dr. Hargrove get her hands on it," Max said. "If she succeeds, the damage could be irreversible."

The siblings gathered closer as Max pointed to another passage in the notebook. "Mom believed the jewel's power was tied to a ritual involving light and symbols. She found references to a specific alignment—something about using the Raven's Heart to open a hidden gateway."

"A gateway to what?" Ava asked.

Max shrugged. "That part isn't clear. But she thought it might be a vault containing lost knowledge or treasures. She wrote here, 'The jewel's power reveals what has been forgotten. But only those who walk the path of truth may see its light.'"

"That sounds like a riddle," Leo said, rolling his eyes.

"It's more than that," Emma said. "It's a warning. The jewel can only be used by someone who's worthy—someone the Warden recognizes as a protector, not a thief."

Max looked at the glowing fragment, his expression troubled. "There's one more thing," he said hesitantly. "The fragment we have—it's only part of the Raven's Heart. Without the other pieces, it's incomplete."

"So Dr. Hargrove still has the rest of it," Emma said, her tone sharp. "And she's planning to use it tonight."

Sophie stood, her fists clenched. "Then we don't have time to sit here talking. If we know where she's going, we need to stop her."

"She's heading for the chamber beneath the Tower," Max said. "The alignment Mom mentioned—it's happening tonight. If she completes the ritual, she might unlock the jewel's full power."

Emma closed the notebook and stood, her expression resolute. "Then we'll stop her. Max, bring the fragment. If the Warden has been helping us so far, it'll help us again."

Ava slipped the notebook into her bag. "We're not just protecting the Tower anymore, are we?"

"No," Emma said. "We're protecting something much bigger."

The siblings prepared quickly, gathering their tools and reviewing their plan. The Raven's Heart wasn't just a legendary artifact—it was a key to unlocking ancient secrets, tied to a power none of them fully understood. And in the wrong hands, it could bring untold destruction.

As they stepped into the night, the Tower loomed ahead, its ancient walls shrouded in shadows. The final confrontation was approaching, and the siblings knew there was no turning back. The Raven's Heart, the Warden of Shadows, and the Tower's fate were all intertwined—and it was up to them to protect it all.

Chapter 27: Breaking In

The White Tower loomed in the darkness, its ancient stones casting long shadows across the moonlit grounds. The Edmondson siblings stood huddled near an overgrown hedge, their breaths visible in the crisp night air. Ahead of them, guards patrolled the entrance to the underground chamber, their movements sharp and deliberate.

"This is going to be tricky," Emma whispered, her eyes scanning the scene. "The guards aren't going to make this easy."

"Not to mention whatever traps are waiting for us inside," Max added, clutching the notebook filled with Ava's deciphered map.

Sophie grinned, already bouncing on the balls of her feet. "Tricky is our specialty."

The siblings formulated their plan quickly. Max and Ava would guide the group using the decoded map, identifying any traps or hidden mechanisms. Sophie, with her knack for agility, would lead the infiltration, scouting ahead and clearing paths where needed. Leo would handle any technical obstacles, and Emma would coordinate their efforts, keeping them focused.

"Everyone ready?" Emma asked, her voice steady.

The siblings nodded, their resolve clear.

"Then let's move."

Phase 1: Evading the Guards

Sophie led the group as they crept closer to the guarded entrance. The guards patrolled in pairs, their flashlights slicing through the shadows. Timing was everything.

"Wait for it," Sophie whispered, crouched low behind a stack of old barrels.

The siblings held their breath as a pair of guards passed by, their footsteps echoing in the stillness. As soon as the guards turned a corner, Sophie darted forward, signalling the others to follow.

"Stay close to the wall," she said, her voice barely audible.

The group moved silently, hugging the shadows. Leo used a small device to intercept the guards' radio chatter, ensuring they stayed ahead of any potential surprises.

"Two more guards coming," he whispered, holding up a hand. The siblings ducked into a recessed alcove, barely avoiding detection.

Once the path was clear, they slipped through the main gate, descending into the depths of the Tower.

Phase 2: The Traps

The air grew colder as the siblings entered a narrow passageway lined with ancient carvings. Ava consulted her sketchpad, her sharp eyes scanning the walls for clues.

"According to the map, there's a pressure plate ahead," she said, pointing to the floor. "Step on it, and it triggers some kind of mechanism."

"What kind of mechanism?" Sophie asked.

Max shrugged. "It could be anything—spikes, a collapsing ceiling, arrows. You know, the usual."

"Great," Sophie muttered.

Ava knelt down, running her fingers along the edge of the pressure plate. "There's a gap here. If we wedge something into it, we might be able to disarm it."

Leo handed her a thin, sturdy tool from his bag. "Here. Be careful."

Ava worked quickly but meticulously, her hands steady. After a tense moment, she sat back. "Got it. It's disarmed."

The siblings moved forward cautiously, encountering several more traps along the way. Max spotted a tripwire hidden in the shadows, and Sophie deftly leapt over it to secure a safe path for the others. Leo used his toolkit to bypass a hidden lock mechanism, revealing a concealed passage that bypassed a heavily trapped corridor.

Phase 3: The Inner Chamber

After what felt like hours of careful navigation, the siblings reached the final door—a massive, iron-bound barrier etched with glowing symbols.

"This is it," Ava said, her voice hushed. "The chamber where the Raven's Heart is hidden."

"But it's locked," Leo said, examining the door. "And it's not just a normal lock. This thing is ancient and magical."

"Let me see," Max said, consulting the notebook. He flipped to a page with a detailed sketch of the door's symbols. "There's a sequence here—if we press the symbols in the right order, it should open."

Emma nodded. "Then let's get it right. We've come too far to mess this up."

Max studied the symbols, his brow furrowed in concentration. "It's the raven first, then the crown, and then... this one." He pointed to a spiral shape near the bottom of the door.

Emma pressed the symbols in the sequence Max had described. The door groaned and shuddered before swinging open with a resounding thud.

The siblings stepped inside, their flashlights cutting through the darkness. The chamber was vast, its walls lined with intricate carvings that seemed to hum with energy. In the center stood the pedestal, its surface glowing faintly. Resting atop it were the remaining fragments of the Raven's Heart, their combined light illuminating the room.

But their relief was short-lived.

Dr. Hargrove and the security officer stood on the far side of the chamber, their expressions shifting from shock to fury as they spotted the siblings.

"You again," Dr. Hargrove sneered. "You don't know when to quit, do you?"

Emma stepped forward, her voice unwavering. "We're here to stop you. Whatever you're planning, it ends now."

Dr. Hargrove's eyes gleamed with a dangerous intensity. "Oh, you're too late, my dear. The Raven's Heart is mine."

The security officer reached for a device strapped to his belt, but Sophie was faster. She lunged forward, knocking the device from his hand.

"Go!" Emma shouted. "Protect the jewels!"

The siblings spread out, ready to face whatever came next. The final battle for the Raven's Heart had begun, and they were determined to protect the Tower and its secrets at all costs.

Chapter 28: The Thief Revealed

The glow of the Raven's Heart fragments filled the chamber with an eerie light as the Edmondson siblings stood their ground, facing Dr. Evelyn Hargrove and her accomplice. The tension crackled in the air, thick with the weight of betrayal and unfinished business.

"You've been meddling in things you don't understand," Dr. Hargrove said, her voice cold and steady as she stepped forward. "Do you have any idea what this jewel truly is?"

Emma clenched her fists. "We know enough to understand that it doesn't belong to you."

"Belong?" Hargrove's lips curled into a faint smirk. "The Raven's Heart belongs to no one. It's a tool, a key to unlock the secrets of the Tower and beyond. And in the right hands, it can change everything."

"Your hands, you mean," Sophie shot back, her eyes narrowing.

"You lied to us," Max said, his voice trembling with anger. "You pretended to help us, but you were using us to get what you wanted."

Dr. Hargrove raised an eyebrow, her smirk widening. "Of course, I was. You're intelligent, resourceful—and, most importantly, naïve. You did exactly what I needed, leading me to the Raven's Heart and solving the puzzles I didn't have time for. So thank you for your assistance."

Emma stepped forward, her voice cutting through the tension like a blade. "Why are you doing this, Evelyn? You're not just a thief. You've dedicated your life to the Tower's history. Why betray it now?"

Dr. Hargrove's smile faded, replaced by something darker. "Because the Tower's history is incomplete—a shadow of what it once was. Do you know how many secrets lie buried beneath these stones? How much knowledge has been lost because no one dared to look deeper? The Raven's Heart isn't just a jewel—it's a gateway to that knowledge. I'm not stealing it. I'm claiming it for what it's meant to be."

"And you're willing to destroy the Tower to do it," Max said.

"If that's the price, then so be it," Hargrove replied, her voice cold.

As the siblings processed her words, the security officer moved toward the pedestal, reaching for the Raven's Heart fragments.

"Stop him!" Emma shouted.

Sophie lunged forward, knocking the officer off balance. He stumbled, but Dr. Hargrove moved quickly, pulling a small, intricate device from her satchel and fitting it into a groove on the pedestal.

"What is she doing?" Ava whispered, clutching Emma's arm.

"She's activating it," Max said, panic rising in his voice. "If she combines the fragments, the Raven's Heart's full power will be unleashed!"

The room seemed to darken as the fragments began to hum, their glow intensifying. Dr. Hargrove's face lit up with triumph as she manipulated the device, connecting the fragments together. The air grew heavy, vibrating with an unseen energy.

"You don't know what you're unleashing!" Emma shouted.

"I know exactly what I'm unleashing," Hargrove replied, her voice steady. "A future where the past isn't hidden—where the truth is finally revealed."

Before Hargrove could complete the connection, the ghostly figure of the Warden of Shadows appeared, its translucent form blocking her path. The air crackled with energy as the Warden raised its hand, its voice booming through the chamber.

"YOU ARE NOT WORTHY."

The ground trembled, and Hargrove staggered backward, her face pale but defiant. "You think you can stop me? You're nothing more than a relic—just like this place."

The Warden turned toward the siblings, its hollow eyes locking onto Emma. Its voice softened, resonating with an almost human tone. "The Raven's Heart belongs to those who protect the truth, not twist it for power."

Emma stepped forward, her gaze unwavering. "Then help us stop her. She doesn't care about the Tower—only what she can take from it."

The Warden nodded, its form flickering as it moved to shield the fragments. Dr. Hargrove glared at Emma, her composure finally cracking.

"You have no idea what you're doing," she hissed. "The Tower's secrets will remain buried because of your childish ideals."

"Some secrets are meant to stay buried," Emma replied.

With the Warden's help, the siblings sprang into action. Max and Ava worked quickly to disarm the device Hargrove had placed on the pedestal, while Leo distracted the security officer, who had recovered and was advancing again. Sophie tackled Hargrove, forcing her away from the Raven's Heart.

"You're done," Sophie said, pinning Hargrove against the wall.

Hargrove sneered. "You think you've won? This is far from over."

As the siblings secured the fragments and the device, the Warden raised its hand again, summoning a barrier of light around the pedestal. The Raven's Heart dimmed slightly, its power contained once more.

Dr. Hargrove and her accomplice were restrained, their plans thwarted. The chamber fell silent, save for the faint hum of the fragments.

The Warden turned to Emma, its form flickering. "The Tower's guardians have prevailed. The truth remains safe—for now."

"What happens to the Raven's Heart?" Emma asked.

"It will remain here," the Warden said. "Protected by those who honour its purpose."

With a final, lingering look, the Warden dissolved into the air, leaving the siblings alone in the quiet chamber.

As the siblings emerged into the night, Dr. Hargrove and the security officer in custody, Emma looked at her family, her heart swelling with pride and relief.

"We did it," she said.

"But at what cost?" Max asked, his gaze lingering on the Tower's ancient walls.

Emma placed a hand on his shoulder. "At the cost of protecting what matters. The Tower, its history, and the truth."

For the Edmondson siblings, the adventure had ended—but the legacy of the Raven's Heart, and the lessons they had learned, would stay with them forever.

Chapter 29: The Ghost's Past

The Raven's Heart fragment pulsed faintly as the Edmondson siblings sat in the dimly lit chamber beneath the Tower. Dust still hung in the air from their narrow escape, but their thoughts were now on something far older, more haunting. The ghost—the Warden of Shadows—had saved them multiple times, its presence more than just a curse or a guardian.

"There's more to it," Max said, flipping through Thomas Grey's diary. "The ghost isn't just a random spirit tied to the Raven's Heart. It has a story—a purpose."

Emma leaned forward, her expression tense. "What did you find?"

Max tapped a passage near the end of the diary, where the handwriting grew shaky. "Here: 'The Warden is no myth. It was once one of us—a loyal guard betrayed by those they trusted most. Falsely accused, they were condemned to death, their spirit bound to the Tower by the Raven's Heart, cursed to protect what they died defending.'"

Ava's eyes widened. "The ghost was a guard? That's... awful."

"It makes sense, though," Sophie said, her voice quieter than usual. "That's why it keeps appearing around the Raven's Heart. It's not just protecting it—it's protecting its honour."

Max flipped to another page, his excitement growing. "Listen to this: 'The guard's name was Elias Ravenscroft. They were no ordinary sentinel, but the alchemist who forged the Raven's Heart itself. Accused of theft and treachery by their jealous peers, they were executed within the Tower walls. The Raven's Heart, created to protect the Tower's treasures, instead became their eternal prison.'"

"Wait," Leo said, frowning. "The ghost isn't just a guard—it's the person who created the Raven's Heart?"

Emma nodded, her expression grim. "They were framed, betrayed by the very people they trusted to protect. And now they're stuck here, tied to the jewel they made."

The siblings fell silent, the weight of the revelation settling over them. The ghost wasn't just a figure of fear—it was a victim, caught in an endless loop of guarding the Tower and its secrets.

Ava broke the silence, her voice trembling. "That's why it saved us. It knows we're trying to protect the Raven's Heart, not steal it."

"And it knows what betrayal looks like," Sophie added, her fists clenched. "Hargrove and her goon are just like the people who betrayed it centuries ago."

Max nodded. "But the diary says something else. Elias's spirit isn't just protecting the Raven's Heart—it's searching for redemption. If the truth about their betrayal is revealed, the curse might finally be lifted."

Emma stood, her resolve hardening. "Then that's what we have to do. We'll stop Hargrove and protect the Raven's Heart, but we'll also uncover the truth about Elias Ravenscroft. It's the only way to bring them peace."

"How do we do that?" Leo asked. "The people who betrayed them are long dead."

"The truth is in the Tower," Max said. "The records, the symbols, the carvings—they're all part of Elias's story. If we can piece it together, we might be able to prove their innocence."

The siblings split up, scouring the hidden chambers for anything that could shed light on Elias's story. Ava's sharp eyes caught faint inscriptions in the stone walls, detailing Ravenscroft's achievements as a trusted alchemist and guard. Max found old records in a forgotten archive, hinting at a conspiracy among Ravenscroft's peers, who had fabricated the theft to cover their own crimes.

By the time they regrouped, they had assembled the pieces of a centuries-old puzzle: Elias Ravenscroft had been framed by rival guards jealous of their skill and knowledge. The betrayal had been covered up, and Elias's name erased from the Tower's official history.

As the siblings presented their findings in the chamber, the Raven's Heart fragment glowed brighter, its pulsing energy filling the room. The ghost appeared, its form flickering but more solid than ever. Its hollow eyes fixed on Emma, and for the first time, it spoke clearly.

"You have uncovered the truth," it said, its voice both sorrowful and grateful. "I was Elias Ravenscroft, loyal to the Tower until the end. Betrayed by those I called comrades, my spirit was bound to this place, cursed to protect what I could no longer hold dear."

Emma stepped forward, holding the fragment. "We know what happened to you, Elias. You were innocent. And we'll make sure everyone knows it."

The ghost's form wavered, its voice softening. "The truth is all I ever sought. If my name can be restored, my spirit may finally rest."

The siblings worked quickly, leaving no stone unturned as they uncovered documents, carvings, and artifacts that confirmed Elias's innocence. They presented their findings to the Tower's officials, ensuring that the truth was recorded and shared.

As the story of Elias Ravenscroft spread, the ghost appeared one final time. The chamber glowed with an otherworldly light as the Warden of Shadows stepped forward, its form more human than ever.

"Thank you," it said, its voice steady and full of peace. "You have freed me."

The Raven's Heart pulsed brightly before dimming, its energy contained. The ghost faded slowly, leaving the siblings in awe.

Emma turned to her siblings, her voice steady but emotional. "We did it. We saved the Tower, and we saved Elias."

Ava wiped a tear from her cheek. "And now the ghost can finally rest."

Max looked at the Raven's Heart, its glow faint but calm. "And the Tower is safe—for now."

The siblings left the chamber together, their bond stronger than ever. The Tower's secrets were no longer a burden but a legacy, one they had protected and honoured. Elias Ravenscroft's story had been restored, and with it, a piece of history had been made whole.

Chapter 30: Recognition and Mystery

The sun rose over the Tower of London, casting its golden light across the ancient stones as the Edmondson siblings emerged from the underground chambers. Their faces were weary but triumphant, and their hearts were full from the weight of what they had accomplished. The Raven's Heart fragments were safe, the Tower's secrets protected, and Elias Ravenscroft's name restored to history.

Tower staff and officials had gathered in the courtyard, their faces a mix of relief, curiosity, and scepticism. The siblings handed over their carefully gathered evidence, including Thomas Grey's diary, the fragments of the Raven's Heart, and the documents proving Elias's innocence.

"Everything we've found is here," Emma said, addressing the group. "Elias Ravenscroft wasn't a thief. They were framed by those who envied them, and they sacrificed everything to protect the Tower."

Chief Warden Tyndall, the head of the Tower's security, stepped forward, his stern face softening as he examined the evidence. "You've done an incredible thing," he said, his voice carrying across the courtyard. "The Tower owes you more than words can express. You've not only saved its treasures but also uncovered a piece of its history long forgotten."

Several guards nodded in agreement, murmuring their appreciation. The siblings exchanged small, proud smiles.

Dr. Evelyn Hargrove and her accomplice, the security officer, had been taken into custody after their failed plot. The Tower's officials promised a full investigation into their actions and the thefts.

"You'll be remembered for this," Warden Tyndall said, looking at the siblings. "Your courage and dedication have ensured that the Tower's legacy remains intact."

But not everyone in the crowd seemed convinced. A middle-aged historian folded his arms, his brow furrowed. "And what of this ghost you claim to have seen?" he asked, his tone sceptical. "The Warden of Shadows? A convenient story to explain what cannot be proven."

Max stepped forward, holding the diary tightly. "The ghost isn't just a story. It's a part of the Tower's history—of Elias Ravenscroft's legacy. It protected the Raven's Heart and saved our lives."

The historian scoffed. "Perhaps your minds played tricks on you in those dark chambers. Or perhaps the 'ghost' was nothing more than a figment of your imagination, inspired by the legends."

"Figment?" Sophie said, crossing her arms. "It wasn't a figment when it saved me from getting crushed. And it wasn't imaginary when it stood between us and Hargrove."

Leo smirked. "If the ghost wanted to prove you wrong, it probably would've dropped a rock on your head by now."

The crowd chuckled, breaking the tension. Still, the historian shook his head, unconvinced. "Legends are legends for a reason," he muttered, walking away.

As the crowd dispersed, the siblings stood together, watching the bustle of the Tower return to normal. Tourists began arriving, oblivious to the incredible events that had unfolded just beneath their feet.

Emma turned to her siblings, her voice thoughtful. "Not everyone will believe what we saw. But that doesn't matter. We know the truth—and so does Elias."

Ava looked at the Raven's Heart fragments, now carefully sealed in a protective case. "Do you think the ghost is really gone?"

Max nodded. "Elias's story is complete now. Their name is restored, and their spirit is at peace."

"But the Tower still has secrets," Sophie said, glancing at the ancient stones. "Who knows what else is hidden in these walls?"

Emma smiled, her eyes twinkling with a mixture of pride and wonder. "Maybe that's for someone else to discover. For now, we've done our part."

As the siblings prepared to leave the Tower, Warden Tyndall approached them one last time. "Your family's reputation for uncovering mysteries is well deserved," he said, shaking Emma's hand. "The Tower is grateful for your bravery—and for your respect for its history."

"It was our honour," Emma said, her voice steady.

Tyndall gave them a rare smile. "Should you ever find yourselves back in London, the Tower will welcome you. After all, it seems you have a knack for uncovering its secrets."

As they walked away, the siblings couldn't help but glance back at the Tower, its imposing silhouette framed against the morning sky.

"Do you think it's really over?" Ava asked, her voice quiet.

Emma placed a hand on her shoulder. "For Elias, it is. But for the Tower? Its mysteries will always endure."

"And maybe," Max said, his gaze lingering on the Raven's Heart, "that's the way it's meant to be."

With a final look, the Edmondson siblings turned toward their next adventure, the Tower of London behind them—but its legacy forever a part of their story.

Chapter 31: A Lesson Learned

The train ride out of London was quiet, the rhythmic clatter of wheels against the tracks providing a soothing backdrop as the Edmondson siblings sat together, each lost in their thoughts. The events at the Tower of London had been nothing short of extraordinary, and the weight of what they had uncovered still lingered in the air between them.

Emma sat by the window, her chin resting in her hand as she gazed at the passing countryside. The golden fields and distant hills were a stark contrast to the cold, shadowy chambers of the Tower. But in the stillness of the journey home, she found herself reflecting on everything they had faced—and what they had learned.

Emma glanced at her siblings. Max was poring over the family notebook, his curiosity still insatiable. Ava was sketching, her focus unwavering as she tried to capture the Raven's Heart and the ghostly Warden in her art. Sophie was tapping her foot to a song only she could hear, her boundless energy temporarily subdued. Leo was tinkering with one of his gadgets, muttering to himself as he tried to fix a stubborn circuit.

Each of them had played a vital role in solving the mystery, and Emma couldn't help but feel proud. But as their leader, she also felt the weight of every decision she'd made—the risks she'd asked them to take, the moments of fear they'd faced together.

She sighed softly, her breath fogging the glass. *Courage isn't about not being afraid,* she thought. *It's about standing firm in the face of fear—and trusting the people by your side.*

The memory of their narrow escape in the collapsing chamber flashed through her mind. Sophie's quick reflexes, Leo's technical expertise, Max's encyclopaedic knowledge, and Ava's sharp eyes had all played a part in saving her—and in solving the mystery.

She smiled faintly, turning toward the group. "You know, we couldn't have done any of this without each other."

Sophie raised an eyebrow. "Obviously. I mean, who else would've kept you all from getting crushed by a falling ceiling?"

Leo smirked. "Or hacked into a 500-year-old security system?"

Max grinned. "Or decoded centuries-old diary entries?"

"And let's not forget the sketching," Ava added with a playful shrug. "Crucial."

Emma chuckled, her heart swelling with affection for her siblings. "I'm serious. We all brought something different to the table, and that's what made us unstoppable. If any one of us hadn't been there, we might not have made it."

Her thoughts drifted to the ghost of Elias Ravenscroft. Their courage and sacrifice had inspired her, not just as a leader but as a person. Elias had faced betrayal, loss, and an eternity of guarding a treasure they could never truly hold. And yet, they had protected the Tower, even in death.

"What Elias did…" Emma began, her voice quieter. "It reminded me that doing the right thing isn't always easy. It takes courage to stand up for the truth, even when no one else believes you."

Max looked up from the notebook, his expression thoughtful. "You're right. They didn't just protect the Raven's Heart—they protected their honour, even after everything they went through."

"And now, because of us, people know their story," Ava said, her voice filled with quiet pride.

Emma reached for the notebook, flipping to one of the pages that had guided them through their adventure. The drawing of the Raven's Heart glowed faintly in her memory, its significance far greater than its beauty.

"We've been through so much," Emma said, her voice steady. "But this wasn't just about solving a mystery or stopping a thief. It was about protecting something bigger than ourselves—history, honour, and the truth."

Sophie leaned back in her seat, her grin mischievous. "So what's next, fearless leader? Another cursed treasure? An ancient city of gold?"

Leo snorted. "As long as there aren't any more collapsing ceilings, I'm in."

Emma smiled, her gaze shifting to the rolling hills outside. "Whatever comes next, we'll face it together. That's the real lesson here. No matter how impossible something seems, if we trust each other and work as a team, we can handle anything."

The train rattled on, carrying the siblings away from the Tower and toward their next adventure. Though the Raven's Heart was behind them, its legacy—and the lessons they had learned—would stay with them forever.

For Emma, courage wasn't just about facing danger. It was about believing in herself and in the people she cared about. It was about standing up for what was right, even when the odds seemed insurmountable.

And as the leader of the Edmondson siblings, she knew one thing for certain: together, there was nothing they couldn't achieve.

Disclaimer

This book is a work of fiction. While it is inspired by real historical locations, such as the Tower of London, and references certain historical elements, all characters, events, and specific details of the mystery are purely fictional. Any resemblance to actual persons, living or deceased, is purely coincidental.

The depiction of ghosts, curses, and other supernatural phenomena in this story is intended for entertainment purposes only and does not reflect any claims about their existence in real life. Similarly, the portrayal of the Tower of London's security measures, historical artifacts, and procedures has been imagined for narrative purposes and should not be taken as accurate or reflective of the actual site.

The author encourages readers to explore the fascinating history of the Tower of London through reputable historical sources. This book aims to spark curiosity and imagination while celebrating the thrill of adventure and the enduring power of teamwork and family.

Enjoy the adventure!